Emmanuelle Arsan is the [...]
Eurasian – Maryat Rollet [...]
of the French delegation [...]
served at a diplomatic post [...]
view of the human sexual [...]
tional fame and has turned [...]
both sides of the Atlantic. Distinguished critic Françoise
Giroud of *L'Express* wrote of her that she 'preaches the
"erotic revolution" as seriously as others preach in today's
China "the cultural revolution".' The bestselling *Emmanuelle*
novels have been turned into films that have broken box-
office records all over the world and set new standards for
the erotic cinema.

EMMANUELLE ARSAN

Nea
A Young Emmanuelle

Translated from the French
by Celeste Piano

GRAFTON BOOKS
A Division of the Collins Publishing Group

LONDON GLASGOW
TORONTO SYDNEY AUCKLAND

Grafton Books
A Division of the Collins Publishing Group
8 Grafton Street, London W1X 3LA

Published by Grafton Books 1978
Reprinted 1978, 1979, 1980, 1982, 1983, 1985, 1986, 1988, 1989

ISBN 0-586-21040-7

Printed and bound in Great Britain by
Collins, Glasgow

Set in Times

To be a perpetual assault upon decency. Nothing to fear.
He practises among the blind.

Jean Cocteau: *A Stranger's Diary*

If the woman dare heal without qualifications, she is a witch
and must die.

Jules Michelet: *Witchcraft*

Dear Emmanuelle,

This notebook contains the account of an experience spanning ten years. I may say that it is a rather unusual testimony and should add that it is also my complete life story.

I am a sociologist, so no doubt you will find certain sections too abstract and long, perhaps regretting the absence of those vivid details and that style I admire in your own books, which is what makes them so wonderfully clear.

In any case, should you wish to make public an experience I consider exemplary in many ways, please do not hesitate to cut or rephrase: I know you won't let me down. What matters is the route taken. That suffering undergone or inflicted before Nea wins the right to talk without remorse to Emmanuelle. If I hand over these pages to yourself, and through you offer them to all those who have learned to know themselves better, it's because bigots still exist. They love virtue as an ogre does his children. Hell-bent on punishing themselves, they want their contemporaries to get their fair share of those miseries and burdens which thin their own blood and turn their guts to acid.

I was their child and heir. For a time I gratified them. But another flame consumed me. Had they felt its heat they would have called it sin.

Later, I knew it could warm rather than burn and then it was called happiness.

I received Nea's letter and manuscript in October 1974. She is right on all counts. Her experiences deserve to be read. She somewhat exaggerates her literary shortcomings, but all the same I have respected her wish. I have therefore deleted some reflections which would probably fascinate doctors and sociologists. As for her style, she has a tone quite her own: her analyses and ideas about love differ considerably from mine, but we find common ground in our mutual respect for truth and freedom. It is for the reader to decide between us and to detect what is Nea's in these pages and what they owe to Emmanuelle.

Emmanuelle Arsan

PART ONE

MY SORROW'S AIM

As if, alas, I waited day by day
For you, the loved one, and your glad return,
There did I set my sorrow's aim

Louise Labé

Chapter I

THURSDAY BACK TO SCHOOL

*I am telling you once again and do so for the last time. Let the
blood soak through, let the blood soak through!*

St Marie-Madeleine Pazzi (*Ecstasies, Book II*)

For the time being I do not seek a key; I no longer want to
and can supply none. Memories, facts and impressions,
sometimes a retrospective reflection, are all that occur to
me. Above all no criticisms, still less judgments. An opening
contradiction: my Christian name or names – Naomi-Anna.
My mother at once called me Nea ...

That morning I was lying naked on my bed. I wasn't
thinking about breakfast (it was not yet seven a.m.) but
about the first taste of that first Thursday of the new school
term.

Every year at the start of October in our glass and stainless steel Neuilly apartment, Mother persists in cooking up
in a copper dish the preserved fruit to last us through the
winter: fifty jars each covered with a disc of greaseproof
paper dipped in brandy and hermetically sealed with cello-
phane and a rubber band. I prefer the shop jams, but in
order not to upset mother I remark that there's nothing to
equal home-made. Thinking about this preserve triggers off
everything else – visions of the family house, sold after
various obscure territorial squabbles, of which I heard only
snatches without quite understanding their cause or
significance. With eyes closed I could see a procession of
stately furniture now disused, suites, bookcases, billiard-
tables, and those faded damasks that seemed the very tex-

13

ture of the days, and the jonquil room where the thirty volumes of *La Mode Illustrée* that had belonged to great-grandmother Auboyer were kept.

When nude I can almost always call to mind memories in this way, and produce feelings that make me breathe the faster, make me feel like singing or crying hot tears. Thinking of summer, for instance, can depress me.

But this morning I do not feel like being sad. I open my eyes, pull the sheet back over me and burrow down the bed. Then I change my mind and hop into my slippers. I rush to the basin, brush my teeth and wash quickly and thoroughly.

I'm going to do my homework. Grammar today. I'm strong on grammar although I despise the stuff. Anyhow I've had some of my best marks for it, and the teachers and even my classmates are amazed at my facility. I know that all it takes to sort out a parsing exercise is a goodish memory. But on the other hand no one realizes the trouble I take to word the solution of a problem stylishly. *That* makes me far prouder, but those very girls who are good at French claim to despise Maths. So I keep my touch of snobbery to myself and go on seeking a perfection that annoys everyone, including and especially my Maths teacher. This whole realm of the intellect fills me with confusion. What seems easy to me dazzles teachers and parents: what I blunder over seems to them insignificant. Are they more ignorant than I imagine, and my parents more naïve? In a couple of minutes I draft an interminable sentence comprising four or five past participles agreeing with the subject, as direct object, or remaining invariable. I fit three examples into two tenses – full marks.

Finished. I'm quite lightheaded, ecstatic.

The apartment stirs. Mother has left her room at least twice. She is no longer in slippers. Her heels click over the small copper slats of the spiral staircase connecting the two floors of the duplex. As for father, he lies doggo. He hates the morning's domestic bustle, but since his car accident two years ago he no longer goes to the office. His manager comes regularly to see him, as do the department heads of his plumbing suppliers business. So in order to avoid his wife and not to have to give his opinion on the day's menus, he shuts himself up from the crack of dawn. Everyone knows he has nothing to do except read the paper but no one would dare say right out that his day's work is a sham. Anyhow, he has become unbeatable at solving the most difficult crosswords.

Dolores, the new Spanish maid who helps Marcelle, is in the linen-room ironing. The smell of warm linen mingles with that of the preserve, which lingers everywhere despite the perfect air-conditioning and kitchen extractors.

I decide to wake my sister Suzanne. I go slowly to the end of the corridor, opposite our parents' two rooms.

Suzanne half opens her eyes.

'Nea? Will you bring my breakfast?'

'Coming up.'

I shut the door and dart off to the stairs, where I bump straight into Marcelle.

'Oh sorry Marcelle! Will you help me get Suzanne's tray ready?'

'If you think I have the time, Mademoiselle Nea . . .'

Marcelle jibs at the idea, but half turns towards the kitchen none the less.

Tray balanced on one hand, I return to Suzanne's room.

'Thanks,' my sister says.

I do like my sister and the movements she makes to install herself more comfortably against her two pillows – the large white one bordered with pink, and the other smaller one for her head, all pink except for its lime-green lace embroidery.

'What a lovely dahlia! You, Nea . . .?'

'Yes, I nicked it from a bouquet probably sent by that poovy gasbag who had dinner here yesterday evening.'

'Has Maurice arrived?'

15

'It's much too early!'

Maurice is Suzanne's fiancé. They are going to get married in October. That's another inexpressible satisfaction which makes my heart beat foolishly: Suzanne engaged, Suzanne in a man's arms, Suzanne swooning with love.

Although they keep quiet in front of me, I've guessed that father is on Maurice's side but mother, without admitting it openly, doesn't like him. Maurice is an engineer or lawyer, I'm not quite sure which. He's some sort of adviser with a chemicals firm and soon he'll be head of a sector (or is it section?) of this company.

'Basically your Maurice is just a salesman,' says mother bitterly to Suzanne.

'No mother, he's a commercial technician ...'

Father supports her:

'Nowadays the back-up areas predominate. Selling a service ...'

I take it in but don't follow.

Maurice, it must be said, has nothing of the commercial traveller about him. Mother is wrong. He has downy blond hairs along his long arms. I saw him in shirt sleeves this last summer. His face, a matt white, is always impassive. His lips are very clearly defined, like a statue's, as if etched, but rather pale. He has narrow cheekbones and around his grey eyes there are innumerable tiny wrinkles. To make me laugh, puffing out his cheeks like balloons, he takes on the look of a huge, blinking owl.

Suzanne was twenty-one six months ago. Sometimes she and mother argue. Mother tells her off:

'It's true you're an adult, so don't expect me to take up your dresses or tidy your cupboards for you any more. I also like lounging about on the settee with a good novel, you know ...'

Without even pausing for breath I descend to the ground

16

floor and prowl around the gleaming kitchenware and the all-purpose cooker that runs the central heating and the hot water supply. Mother has temporarily entrusted her jam-making tureen to Marcelle, whom I ask for a cup of cocoa. Marcelle protests but serves it, grumbling, with almost a whole *baguette* sliced down the middle, buttered and salted just how I like it.

I climb back to my room. The morning is chilly but it looks as if it will be a fine day. The street is still and silent, the dew has already evaporated from the balcony geraniums. The flies have that clumsy autumnal heaviness and hit the glass with an unhealthy buzzing. Thanks to the double-glazing on the big windows the house is just as quiet when there are cars outside: the noise of their engines can't be heard.

I sit down in front of my orange plastic desk. I open a drawer, take out my green leather diary and cross off a date from the calendar on the first page. In exactly one week I shall be sixteen. Mother is giving me a camera, Aunt Aline the final volumes of a bound set of Alexandre Dumas – forty books in all, which she's been giving me in instalments over two years. Money from father, which will be set aside with what I've saved to buy a motor scooter. I've worked out that I'll probably be able to pay for it all in one go, via a small loan added to father's present. Suzanne can easily help me out there. By asking father straight away for the money he's certainly planning to give me, and touching Suzanne for a loan, maybe I can even muster the cash today, order the bike and have it actually on my birthday. Fair enough.

I put away my diary and get out my textbook. There are certain rituals I like. I feel a bit like those nuns at Sainte-Marie who decorate the altar, meticulous and pious. I flirt with myself in the garden of a good conscience. Whereas all the girls complain of having too much homework and too many lessons, I am almost a week ahead with the set work. No one pushes me. Every evening I tell approving parents that I've done two lots of English translation before lunch and an essay in the afternoon. Aunt Aline, who always lunches here on Thursdays, frets:

'This little lady works too much. She doesn't need to overdo things.'

'No no,' says mother. 'Let her, she's so gifted it comes easily to her.'

I like to do well.

Suzanne is sweet, she has lovely white breasts with very dark nipples encircled by big brownish rings. My nipples are pink and it's almost as if the little areolae surrounding them are a bit less white than the rest of my skin. But more than anything they are small and pointed. Suzanne's are velvety and rounded like real breasts. When she talks loudly or leans forward they quiver gently. In vain I bend over my washbasin, stripped to the waist, hunching my shoulders forward: my own breasts always keep looking like little ferrety snouts. They don't seem feminine to me. I tease Suzanne mercilessly about her arse, her big bum, though really I begrudge her it. She has truly voluptuous buttocks. I would honestly love to touch them, I'd just love to caress them. Do lovers caress each other's buttocks?

Mother takes me to task for my remarks, which she considers far too crude. Suzanne just laughs and settles back into the nearest available armchair to read or listen to a record.

'If Maurice rings, tell him to wait for me in the sitting-room,' Suzanne says, getting up.

She doesn't like to rush, and anyhow mother brought her up with the idea that it's a good move to keep men waiting.

Suzanne has taken off her nightdress and is stretching. We've each had our own rooms for some years now and we

18

rarely undress in front of one another. Yet I always fix things so I'm there when, for example, Suzanne is having a bath or wants to change. I like to see her black fleece with its tight curls beneath that slight fold at the base of the stomach, as in Titian's paintings of nudes. I'm ashamed to see her naked, but I like this feeling of shame. The down over my pubis is only a silky shadow on lips that still seem childish. Suzanne's triangle encroaches a little upon her thighs; it is as thick and resilient as a moquette rug.

Suzanne disappears into the bathroom at the very moment the front-door bell rings. I run to answer it. It's Maurice. Seeing him there, calm, absent-minded, I start slightly, for suddenly the image of Suzanne naked, of her buttocks and especially her black triangle is somehow superimposed upon that of Maurice, whom my eyes have promptly undressed also. I've actually seen him naked in real life, last summer, one day when he was pulling on his swimming trunks near the pool. The small changing hut with a basin and showers hadn't been built then. He thought he was alone and I saw him, saw his sex, long, thick, disgusting, his thick sex hanging between his legs. The sight of this thick disgusting sex affected me in such a way that I can't understand Suzanne's attitude. Obviously they must both rub against each other, but quite honestly I don't know that I'd rather have that odd sort of stick instead of a bush. Maybe if men had only a bush, like Suzanne's, it would be nicer to rub against them. But I'm not sure about *that* machine, though I certainly like looking at statues, especially Greek ones. The men there have nice cocks, not horrid great clubs. They're attractive things, really more like a small bird in its nest, with the balls all tight and round and gathered under the sex – far prettier. But all the same, not as nice as a black triangle, small and velvety and bushy.

'Maurice! Suzanne told me you're to wait for her in the sitting-room. She'll be ready in a quarter of an hour at the most.'

19

And what about father? Does he too, I wonder, try to feel up mother's breasts, belly and triangle? Or is he living alone in his room because she won't let him do so any more? He'd be hurt. Perhaps he doesn't like women. I know there are homosexuals who don't like to see women around, they love other men and look at naked men. But homosexuals have rather high voices and wriggle about like women. Father's not like that. Anyway now I come to think of it, I've heard him joke now and again about queers and queens and that means he isn't. The truth is, mother and father are old. They don't care about sex and all that. It's like going to bed late: they don't realize how lucky they are to be able to stay up whenever they like, or see each other naked if they want without anyone taking offence. Yet perhaps I too, who want to go to bed at midnight every night, would grow used to it in the long run, and maybe in due course seeing a lovely tufted triangle would do nothing for me.

Aunt Aline has come to lunch and she's worrying away:

'Nea doesn't look well, really, I'm sure she's working too hard ...'

'What are you fussing for?' mother interrupts, irritated. 'The child is as fit as a fiddle. If she didn't spend hours reading in bed every night ...'

'That's not fair, mother, last night I turned the light out at eleven ...'

'Nea looks lily-white and rose-pink to me,' says Maurice to calm things down.

I look at him and blush. Quite soon he'll be touching Suzanne's breasts for sure.

'And why not an alabaster neck or teeth like a string of pearls,' I retort crossly, feeling annoyed and shrugging.

I don't know why, but sometimes Maurice irritates me.

'Anyway, I don't like this funny autumn weather.'

'It certainly is close,' Aunt Aline says. 'This cold veal and rice salad was a good idea,' she adds.

'What I do like,' mother comments, 'is our nice Fantanches mineral water . . .'

When Grandma's house was sold, mother, by her sheer persistence, succeeded in inserting a clause in the sale contract entitling us during her lifetime to draw the fresh spring water from the park. Once a week the messenger boy from father's firm takes time off and fills four demijohns with this celebrated mineral water and brings it back. It's drunk religiously here at home and is something of a ritual, rather like the preserve. And owing to this water, it appears, we're never ill, or if we are, that's because we've just not drunk enough of it.

Maurice and father have embarked upon a long discussion about productivity. I'm listening. My strong point in essays is using their sort of words, ones not usually associated with school. I show them off loftily, store them away in my memory. In class they make my reputation. 'Follow Nea's example, she knows how to use precisely the right word . . .'

At home we don't usually have a siesta hour. But on Thursdays, perhaps because I'm at home then and never have homework hanging over me, I get the impression that I upset normal daily routine. Mother claims she doesn't want to abandon me and, instead of going out shopping, gets stuck into all sorts of time-consuming chores in the flat, so that I see even less of her than usual. Once she's begun, nothing can stop her. She plunges into a cupboard in which are stacked old oddments and scraps of materials accumulated over the last twenty years, and my presence scarcely registers with her. Father, as is his wont, shuts himself up in his study, but in the afternoons, instead of doing his crosswords, slyly watches the three o'clock TV serial or reads detective novels.

'What about going to lie down for once, Nea my pet,' says Aunt Aline.

I seize the opportunity to escape. My window faces west and the afternoon sun is flooding through. I pull the curtains. The darkness will recreate the clammy shade of the holidays.

After closing the door I can distinguish the family's footsteps – mother's, father's slightly heavy and hesitant tread, Suzanne's lithe glide. I'm listless. Aunt Aline has gone. As for Maurice he's probably said he has a report to read – he generally does. Being a 'business consultant' he isn't tied to office hours, and theoretically visits his clientèle throughout the day. Since he fell in love with Suzanne, however, I don't know if his business is going well, but the fact is that he wangles things so he can stay at our place for entire afternoons. In our family we hate engaged couples necking. So Maurice thought up this pretext of reports to read. Father considers it quite all right for him to go ahead and invade our privacy like this. As for mother, she's always making surprised references to the rare understanding of Maurice's employers and dropping crude hints about the way the engaged pair really spend the time when left unchaperoned in the flat. More than once Suzanne has got furious with mother and her unpleasant comments. Anyway, the moment they reckon they're out of range of our curiosity, Maurice sneaks into Suzanne's room. I've seen them. Outside, there runs a fire escape that skirts the upper floor of the flat at balcony level, right past the window of my sister's room.

Of course Suzanne hadn't pulled her curtains, because she never does anything thoroughly, and without their seeing me I could climb on to the fire ladder and crane my neck in order to see them lying on the bed. On that occasion I felt sure she had taken off her skirt and knickers and that he was staring at her fleecy bush and stroking it. She was moaning and I knew quite well why, since I indulge in the same game in bed, with my hand. He had opened the fly of his trousers, and I couldn't really see him properly, certainly not his prick. I could only make out the silhouette of what looked (from the angle at which I was peering) like his pubic hair. I guessed or had the impression that they were quarrelling down there.

Maurice would have been trying to sleep with Suzanne. She hadn't wanted to and was telling him to clear out. It wasn't hard to understand that she was scared lest one of the family might come in at the wrong moment.

I was annoyed anyhow, because I'd have liked to know at last exactly how a man and a woman make love. It seemed simple in theory. But I didn't quite understand why the fact that a man holds the woman close should make them both experience sensations stronger than those I give myself at night, by playing with myself before going to sleep. The sensations are obviously far stronger, since everyone wants to do it. If not, they'd be quite happy, as I am, with the delightful nocturnal encounters with exploratory fingers, and with rambling dreams and shattering visions.

In spite of the carpeting I always hear Maurice pass my door on his way to see Suzanne. He doesn't dawdle. Now that it's dark and warm I've got the urge. I rapidly undress and fling myself upon the bed, but instead of assuaging this violent craving as I often do, I experience a new desire, a thirst for the sort of pleasure Maurice wanted from Suzanne, and also I remember father's lips against my cheek when I was little, kissing me so softly and tenderly that I would tremble with happiness until the very moment I fell asleep. Tears spring to my eyes, and my finger, instead of briskly rubbing the lips of my pubis, hesitates, scarcely grazes them, and I murmur: 'Maurice, Maurice . . .'

An exquisite torpor overwhelms me. My right hand rests upon my right breast and slides across to the left breast. For the first time in my life I understand the word voluptuousness. This hand can give me something else besides pleasure – voluptuousness, a pleasure beyond pleasure. Until now I only knew how to trigger off a kind of lightning-flash. And yet ... How many times have I remained unsatisfied, my vagina afire, arm and hand aching? I only manage to reach the spasm after an incalculable number of attempts. But today my hand is no longer my hand, it's Maurice's. Maurice: I shut my eyes.

In a louder voice, as if he were here and could hear me, I repeat: 'Maurice, Maurice . . .'

And Maurice appears. He has simply pushed open the door I thought was closed. I am seized with dismay and rage. That damn door with its latch that never works properly . . . And mother always refusing to give me a key. 'A girl of your age doesn't need to lock herself in.'

What does Maurice want? Has he seen me? I pull the sheet up around my neck and give him the dirtiest scowl imaginable. I hate him.

'You can't see a thing in here,' Maurice says. 'Why have you drawn the curtains, in this lovely sunshine? Were you calling me?'

'No . . . Oh . . . yes. Would you please shut the door?'

Maurice does so, his eyes getting used to the darkness.

'Taking a siesta? You might at least have opened the window.'

'I wanted to know . . .' I say, sitting upright, all the time holding the sheet over my breasts.

I think about what I can ask him. Whatever happens he mustn't just leave. He'd think I was an idiot. So I repeat:

'I wanted to know . . . I'm trying to find the formula for a geometry question and I'm really stuck. Do you think you could . . .'

Maurice pulls a face. Suzanne must be waiting for him. Yet after all, he does always say he likes me and I'm so different from Suzanne. He's right, anyhow. *I'd* like to climb Everest and swim across oceans. Whereas Suzanne submits to convention and gives in to mother, who picks on her just the same. They *are* engaged, what's more. So why should mother have the right to forbid Maurice doing things to Suzanne which please her, which give them both pleasure? Like making love together. In fact, why couldn't he make

24

love with me. There's no doubt at all that I'm ready for it!

And what is Maurice thinking about at this very moment? Does he want Suzanne right away, or does he tell himself, perhaps like me, that by making the sheet slip off me he could ... But no, what with my tiny breasts and my little cleft with scarcely a shadow between my legs, he couldn't be interested. Obviously what he really wants are the lovely black curls below Suzanne's belly, into which he can sink. That's the secret perhaps: thickness of hair, Suzanne's I mean, and Maurice's. Maybe it's the gentle rubbing together of these springy fleeces which outdoes that too dry, brief and crude pleasure one gives oneself alone.

'Your sum won't take long?' smiles Maurice.

'Don't worry, you can go to Suzanne as soon as you like ...'

'Right,' says Maurice, sitting on the edge of the bed.

His eyes must have grown accustomed to the murk, for he soon finds my Maths book lying on my desk. He reads the question on the page I show him.

'But it's so easy, Nea!'

I'm looking at Maurice's hand. He has hairs on his finger-joints too. I listen to his voice, a voice somewhat harsh and yet fluid – like sand trickling through the fingers. I like Maths, I've always understood it all easily. Yet I think Maurice is clearer, more lucid than my teacher. The lesson goes on and I'm happy. I even manage to believe that I want to keep Maurice here because of the question. I forget that I've already understood it. Thanks to him, I find I can progress. I put various objections to him, I argue logically, he takes me seriously. I like the smooth click of my little ideas in their bath of intelligence. I'm so intelligent, that all of a sudden I even forget my body. The sheet slides off, I see it slipping. In a flash I tell myself with a hypocrisy I only think about later, that I don't see it. I'm on the point of pulling it back up, but suddenly detect a new tone in Maurice's voice. I think I hear it falter. In the semi-darkness I can sense his eyes are roving. So I change tack. Determined, if suspicious, I leave the sheet where it is – to find out first of all whether he really prefers Suzanne's large white tits. Will he think I have breasts? Seems as though he does, for he's reading faster, stumbling a couple of times. I however, am quite calm now, following his gaze, which again fixes on me – yes, searchingly.

I draw closer to Maurice and without hesitation place my hand on his shoulder. He shudders. I see his stomach tighten and expand above his blue trousers. I see the swelling, that swelling I recognize and which I've already felt against my thigh while dancing during Suzanne's anniversary hop. I know he's no longer in control of it. That I do know about boys. I've been around enough: it sometimes happens to them and every time that's happened with me I've snubbed them. They haven't rubbed against me a second time. My hand descends along Maurice's arm. This gesture is, I feel, for the first time, what might be called a caress. Its sequel will now prove decisive, if he holds my hand I shall carry on. How far? When our fingers meet he takes my hand and shifts awkwardly with a slight laugh.

If he thinks that by just a laugh he can reduce the significance of this gesture, he's mistaken. However, I'm again beset by doubt: here I am in a fix, so I tell myself I must gamble even more. I part my legs. The crumpled sheet is still there and allows me some leeway, a line of retreat, but with a rather brusque movement I push it from the hollow of my thighs.

And now Maurice sees, has to, even if it's only a deeper shadow. If *I* were in Maurice's shoes, I'd be wildly infatuated. How many times have I let my eyes rest on the indentations of a man's swimming trunks or a woman's swimsuit, upon *décolletage* or the swelling under some trousers, yet never dared go further?

It's different for him, he's a man, he knows what to do. If he doesn't do it, it's because he finds nothing about me attractive. Because he doesn't think I'm a woman yet.

'Why do you look at me so oddly?' I ask him.

'You can't see a thing in here,' Maurice replies. 'And how *should* I look at you? What should I be looking at, Nea? What do you mean?'

'I don't mean anything, but I see *you*, so you can surely see me.'

'Nea, let's get back to your question . . .'

I take the book from him, take his hand, which is hot and shaking. I put it to my face and lay it against my cheek and kiss its palm. When I do this he lets out a funny sort of little sigh. So I keep his hand in mine and pull it towards me so his whole body follows like a marionette.

He seems not to realize. I was thinking that he'd know, but he doesn't; on the contrary, you'd almost say that he wanted me to decide. And why not? But I don't know the form: should it be for him or for me? Perhaps a man waits for a sign. Perhaps it's part of this language. I'm told freemasons give a special sign with a finger when shaking hands, so maybe it's the same?

So I draw his hand towards me and place it upon my breast. There, that'll clinch it: if he couldn't care less, well it's as I've feared, my tits might as well not be there and to him I'm only a little girl still. His hand lies flat across my breast. The tiny nipple is as hard as a pearl and his hand not only rests there but moves. Now he is stroking my breast, so he must think it really is a breast. He's put his finger on the hardened nipple – it hurts slightly, it's not really very nice at all because he's pressing too hard – but then *he* must be finding it pleasurable. I waste no time getting his other hand to my breast. He begins again, but he's pressing too hard! He's catching my skin! He . . . I don't know what he wants. But it's strange all the same. If these are caresses . . . I . . . how can I put it . . . I'd imagined things differently. Yet we ought to go on, I've decided.

'Shut the door, we mustn't be disturbed,' I tell him.

27

He gets up dutifully and shuts the door without a word.

'That won't do, mother's liable to come in on any old excuse. I don't want her disturbing our Maths. Would you push the chair under the doorknob so she can't open the door? That's what I usually do. She doesn't like me locking it, she says someone my age doesn't need to lock herself in. She doesn't understand. While I'm working I don't want everybody milling about in here. Come back and sit next to me!'

Maurice does so. He still doesn't say anything. He sits exactly where he did before and stays there. If I'm not careful, he won't make another move. So I take his hand again and guide it towards me, to my breast and stomach. We'll soon find out about my sex appeal. I'm quite happy it's dark. I get the impression that my downy patch is extra thick. I firmly push away the sheet with my foot and put his hand where I usually put my own. Then he starts bearing down, stroking, as I've seen him do to Suzanne, but how can I tell him? It's . . . not quite right. At first he goes much too fast, his finger is far too hard . . . And then what he should do is what one does with a woman. For what he's doing now isn't enough for him when he's with Suzanne, so it shouldn't be all he does with me, and maybe despite my breasts and his hand . . . in that case, perhaps he doesn't really think of me as a woman.

'No, Maurice . . .'

He recoils.

'But Nea, I didn't mean . . . I'm sorry, I lost my head!'

'No Maurice, I'm not angry, quite the opposite. Come back.'

He comes and sits down beside me. I see the bulge in his trousers again and once again think that perhaps it's up to me to make the running. I lay my hand on his thigh. He doesn't move. I touch the swelling under his fly. He stays still, as if he has turned to stone. I'm rather scared. Time passes. Father will soon finish watching his serial, mother will have some crazy scheme she wants to involve me in – there's no time to lose. I undo his belt. Maurice still doesn't move. I slide the zip down, which isn't easy, since zip fasteners are never quite as simple as you'd think. And I feel the bulge there. He has underpants with an opening in the front. I slip my hand into the opening and there it is, how strange! Really I didn't imagine it was like this! Hard, immense. What is he going to do with it? I'm not sure ... So I say to him:

'Maurice, please, come on.'

He gets up, lowers his trousers, takes off his shoes, removes his underpants. His shirt tails flap over his thighs. He has really rather thin thighs, not too nice – long thin thighs. Still, the very fine blond hairs on his arms excite me. I don't know why but these fine fair hairs on Maurice's body, like his owlish stare, make me want to kiss and cuddle him.

'Lie on top of me now.'

He still says nothing at all, but lies on top of me. Nothing, absolutely nothing, happens. I don't feel his bush as I was hoping to do. His hard sex is there between us like a barrier. He has a possessed look, yet possessed with what, I wonder? As for me, I feel nothing except a sort of stomach cramp. He's heavy and he's hurting me. That's better, now he is parting my thighs. I let him do it, for he's certainly had far more experience than I. I must surrender to him completely, or else I'll drop some sort of brick and he'll realize that I'm an absolute beginner.

He spreads my thighs still wider. And that's it. Of course! I knew it all the time. I've seen cats and dogs. And anyway I learned from sex education classes that his sex has to go inside mine.

But I thought that was after one had made love. So therefore you make love at the same time as the sex penetrates you. I wonder how that can be. This big thing, this stick, will never manage to penetrate that very small hole that seems so tight round my finger.

Yet I'm opening up and I'm as wet as when I play with myself. I'm waiting and for me the waiting is always the exciting thing. Besides, I've recently discovered a little trick when I caress myself, which is to keep my hand a few inches from my sex just when I most want it and not stroke myself, sometimes not for several minutes.

My sex is damp. You might almost say 'flooding', whereas sometimes I have so much difficulty, if I caress myself too fast, in producing even a teardrop.

So I'm ready, and there, he's tearing me, ravaging. It hurts. I think I'm going to scream. I think I do scream. No, surely not, because Maurice is on top of me, this time lying absolutely on top, elbows on the bed on both sides of my body. His head in the hollow of my shoulder, he sighs, he is saying something:

'That was marvellous, Nea, Nea my sweet . . . Nea you are a woman now. It was marvellous. You're a woman. Wonderful, it was wonderful, Nea.'

I don't know what was so wonderful about it. I hurt too much. But I do have the certainty I was looking for. I know that what we've just done is love. I even know that during the unbelievable pain I felt, something exploded inside me: I felt spasms within myself and fleetingly experienced a sensation very close to pleasure. Nothing comparable to what I give myself every day; a premonition, however, that I would experience this same pleasure differently hereafter – fully, violently, and with more satisfaction.

'Am I a woman, Maurice?'

'Yes, Nea . . .'

'Am I *your* woman, Maurice?'

Chapter II

MY SISTER, MY MISTRESS

She surrendered herself to me like a toy; I did not abuse my power; instead of subjecting her to my desires, I became her defender.

Chateaubriand: *Posthumous Memoirs*

Maurice has gone. He has once more closed the door behind him.

I have scarcely moved. Once again I am submerged by this slow and lazy afternoon. Softly I run a finger along my thigh. I twist my body a bit in order to see. The already-dried blood gives the effect of a pink wash in a watercolour. But I know that this other liquid with the consistency of egg white is sperm, a man's sperm. I repeat the name knowingly, the forbidden name. No matter how often one says it, parents and teachers still try like mad to lead us to believe that nothing is hidden from us these days – but just you try saying the word 'sperm' as you might 'bread' or 'grass', and you'll soon see the faces they pull! The word sperm is a forbidden word because making love remains forbidden. For a girl of my age anyway.

And even for Suzanne – so she shouldn't give herself airs! Perhaps it's happened to her too, as with me (and I'm happy to say that, 'as with me'), that she's been taken, possessed, loved – I don't know which of these verbs to use. Anyhow, she's certainly been to bed, but that's forbidden to her also. Mother would be furious, father wouldn't believe it. As for boys, I know all too well what they think of a girl who sleeps around. They're the first to take advantage, but the things

31

I've heard them say afterwards! And girls too. Maybe they do some things, but they do so secretly, whereas the ones who are more open get jeered at.

Obviously there's no comparison here with me: Maurice loves me, he told me so.

I'll never forget his strange tone of voice, broken, sad. Until the day I die I will repeat not only the words but also their very intonation: 'It was marvellous Nea, Nea darling, Nea you're a woman now. It was wonderful, wonderful. Nea, Nea, you are a woman.'

It's true, I can repeat every word and above all, discover the meaning of this last phrase. While it was happening I hurt too much, I was happy he'd talked to me as he had, but it was pride rather than anything else. Repeating it to myself now, my whole body tenses once again. Quite naturally my finger moves from my thighs back up to that little cleft that usually I fill with other images, other ideas. But it's no longer my finger, no longer my hand, no longer habit, no longer even Maurice's sex so hard and thick, it's all of Maurice inside me, yet he doesn't hurt me any more.

Darling, darling Maurice. Wonderful, marvellous Maurice. I repeat very softly to myself 'darling' and 'marvellous' because the words give me the keenest possible pleasure in themselves.

Generally I need to recreate a whole scene: a door opens, I enter a room and there a naked man does things to the Spanish chambermaid, for example. He lifts her skirt, squeezes her buttocks, or slides his hand into her bodice so her breasts swell and harden – or, rather, my breasts, small though they are, swell and grow hard.

And then my favourite route is from the nipple, avoiding the navel because my navel is ticklish, down to the stomach. I flex and relax my stomach muscles; feeling this movement of muscles under the skin makes me shudder. Then I play with my bush, trace zigzags and arabesques, holding off for as long as possible. When I can stand it no longer I sink my finger or my whole hand into my sex, which is sometimes so moist that I wet my nightdress or even the sheet.

As I don't want anyone to suspect what I'm doing, I take a small towel from the bathroom before getting into bed, raise my nightdress and place the towel under my hips. Later I replace it in the bathroom so nobody'd ever guess what I've been doing. Today I've taken no special precaution and my bed must look like a battlefield, but that's the least of my worries. My darling wonderful finger does all that is necessary, so rapidly that I don't even have time to think clearly. I'm swept along like a mad thing down a slope where I used to roll when I was little, into the meadow that runs from the house to the river bank. I understand nothing – no, I do understand one thing. Before Maurice, I must have had pleasure: today what I experienced was ecstasy. I understand this at once, immediately grasping the difference between my usual mechanical pleasure and the ecstasy that swallows one up.

I once heard two boys (might as well say men, for they were both at least twenty) use the word 'come'. I caressed myself with this word for almost a month. Yet it was only a word, like 'sex', 'breast', or 'hair', a word that helped me reach my own pleasure. In reality coming is more than just experiencing pleasure. Coming, and this is the difference, only happens to you when you're making love. When Maurice made love to me just now I was surprised and anyway it hurt, otherwise I'd have come, as I usually do. So the climax must just have stayed within me and only now has it happened. I wonder if I'll ever be able to reach it again, without Maurice.

This train of thought is still very clear in my memory, but after it there's a blank. I must have fallen asleep. I remember a sort of heaviness in my legs though my head by contrast feels extraordinarily light. I carefully clean up my sheet and remake the bed. I have a bath in lukewarm water which I gradually run hotter and hotter until the heat becomes unbearable. My temples throb. I feel the sweat trickle down each side of my nose. I want, as I sometimes do, to caress myself again in the bath. Sometimes I find the second time so unexpectedly violent that I'll almost faint. Or else it can happen that I'm left seeking a satisfaction that keeps slipping away from me. Short of breath, I'll give up on these occasions, or attain only a dry sort of relief that leaves me basically unsatisfied and irritable. Now something subtly different happens: from the start I'm utterly without feeling, as if my skin were a thick tissue between my sensations and my real body. Maurice's image is no help to me: on the contrary, I only seem to become drier still.

I get out of the water quickly and wrap myself in a light silk kimono father brought back from a business trip in Japan. That was when he still went on business trips. It was a gift for mother, but she's never worn it – I don't know why. She gave it to me and I love it because it's the most feminine item of clothing I have. It makes me look tall and slim. My hair falls over my shoulders, and if I do my hair in a rather bouffant style I look much older than I am. I borrowed Suzanne's makeup and went to work on myself: eyes, lips and even (as actresses are supposed to do) inside my ears. I'm sure if a man had seen me that day he'd have thought I was quite the sophisticated woman.

But of course I choose times when I'm alone in the flat before making myself up like this. Mother wouldn't like it, she'd consider it an unhealthy pastime. If she only knew, poor thing. Actually, I think she considers everything girls do unhealthy – older ones, I mean. She doesn't even realize! She thinks she's broadminded, and is forever telling us she is, especially when forbidding us to do something or other. In a kimono I feel not only older, but I always get an urge, an aching feeling that goads me straight into an armchair, forcing me to spread my legs and satisfy myself at once, no matter how, hurriedly, unthinking.

I imagine it's the silk, the softness and smell of the silk.

One day I took some perfume from mother's dressing-table. A very strong perfume, containing musk. A very expensive perfume too, which she never uses since she prefers toilet water with a sharp lemon scent. My kimono has remained impregnated with this musky perfume that mingles with my own scent. The mixture makes me think of a film I saw at the Cinémathèque, *Gigi*, adapted from the Colette novel. I imagine that cocottes must have smelt of it, it's the sort of scent that makes you self-aware, conscious of your body.

Physically speaking I don't much like myself. Suzanne is infinitely better off in that respect, but at the moment I forget my shortcomings, dwelling upon my best features. My skin, for instance. I've a very soft skin, rather Chinese in it's fine, pale, matt texture. I've never had pimples or acne, and, what's more, thinking about my skin has the same effect as thinking about my kimono and its scent: it's one of my methods of getting aroused – which is by no means an automatic process. What with school, homework and rushing about here and there I don't really have that much time left over. But I do make sure I masturbate as often as I can: it works out at least once a day.

Suddenly I start seeing Maurice in a different light: he seems far away, he grows blurry – and I embark upon a sort of argument with myself. I'm intelligent, I am now a woman, a woman he has chosen. Suzanne knows nothing of what has happened ... What *will* happen? I feel a curious onset of anger towards Maurice and a surge of fierce love for Suzanne. How could he dare abandon her? Maybe I'm happy or smug about it, but the thought is an unbearable one. It seems to bring me closer to her, against Maurice and his abandonment of her. At least Suzanne must know that *I* love her. He isn't part of the family. She's always found men and always will, as many men as she wants. Maybe, since she's very suggestible, she'll soon resign herself to the idea: certainly *mother* won't be too upset that things between her elder daughter and the 'commercial traveller' won't be going any further ...

I'll bide my time. As far as I'm concerned there's really no problem: I won't be as prudish as Suzanne, who only lets Maurice have little glimpses of flesh, stolen half-kisses in the shadows. Yes, I'll be Maurice's mistress before becoming his wife. But the more I persuade myself that events will inevitably work out thus, the more tenderness I feel towards my sister.

No, what I've been thinking isn't true. I can't bear a grudge against Maurice. You can't resent someone who loves you, and he does love me.

Yet I owe Suzanne something. Not a compensation nor a consolation. Maurice clearly wasn't made for her nor she for him, because I am Suzanne's opposite and Maurice came round to choosing me. What I owe Suzanne is myself. Not a great deal, but it's all I have, I possess nothing except myself. Don't they say that love is a gift of oneself? Now I love no other human being, near or far, as much as I love Suzanne. This daily, invisible love I must reveal to her.

Right, that's it, I'll waste no time. Barefoot I pad down the corridor and noiselessly open the door of her room. She has lowered the blind and has gone to bed. Maurice is not there. I was sure that after having had me he could not, as usual, rejoin his fiancée, or rather his ex-fiancée.

At least that's something learned. I'm not thrilled about it: everything happened just as I felt it would. My logic holds good, and as I see Suzanne, abandoned, open, I stifle a sob. Beside the bed, I take a deep breath.

I stare at her.

That way she has of flinging herself on a bed naked, like the incarnation of laziness and carelessness, without even taking the trouble to turn back the bedcovers decently, without so much as getting her pillows comfortable – that's Suzanne all over, darling marvellous Suzanne. Yes, Suzanne,

36

you are wonderful and marvellous. I murmur the words just like Maurice, not so long ago.

Lying flat on her belly, one leg slightly bent, the other extended, my sister presents to me her beautiful rounded buttocks, her two satin spheres with their imperceptible dimples below the waist, and the shadowy furrow widening between her thighs until in my imagination it quivers darkly, vibrates under my penetrating stare. I lie down beside her, open my kimono and press myself against her body. To start with, she doesn't even notice; then I slip my left arm beneath her head. She raises it slightly as if to make my task easier, but she is still oblivious. My other arm encircles her, joins her own hand lying half open upon her breast, and this hand shifts as if to make room for mine. It's only the hand though, that's so compliant, for Suzanne herself goes on sleeping.

For the first time I find in my palm that darkish nipple, that big brown areola I so envy; the dark nipple which erects like mine, the areola which contracts and trembles.

Almost despite myself, I move my hips forward to press still harder against her: I feel a kind of urgency, an exasperation that I have no maleness, no prick to plunge into her loins. This prick I imagine I ought to have, so as to enter Suzanne as Maurice entered me, would be hard, swollen, twitching, its little vein in relief, its head red . . .

But I stop myself, ashamed, bewildered. Suzanne will think me crazy – or worse still, disgusting. She'll be horrified at my lewdness. I shudder with shame, my heart is almost in my mouth, and the word 'lewdness' hits me like spittle. Another word: always these words I love, which I usually employ so well but which can rebel too, turn against me, brand me for ever, denounce my shame. What will I reply to Suzanne if she says to me: 'Stop those filthy tricks, stop it you slut, what are you doing, you dirty bitch?'

I once heard Jeanne Miallet coming out of the toilet and she said to Michèle Farneaux that she'd heard two girls up to some dirty tricks in the school lavatory next to hers, and she'd recognized the voice of one of them, Louise Ménégaud.

Since that day dirty tricks has always meant, to me, two girls feeling each other up amid assorted lavatory smells. And I must admit to being haunted for months by this image of Louise Ménégaud and another girl up to their dirty tricks, to the point where I'd play with myself. What's more, the wretched Louise Ménégaud wasn't attractive but sly, with round shoulders and a muddy complexion.

But ever since those dirty tricks I was fascinated by her very thin, almost white lips which I could see stuck to my skin like a scar, like the indelible memory of a razor slash.

Father has a set of razors. A lovely mahogany box lined with deep purple velvet, containing seven old-fashioned cut-throat razors. Each broad blade is inlaid in gold and the ivory handles, yellowed with age, are worn so smooth that they seem to have been polished by the hand which held them. I must have been about seven or eight when I got hold of one of them and sustained a nasty cut on the palm of my left hand, which I'd been playfully tickling.

Now, completely immobile, I sense that Suzanne is continuing my earlier movement, on her own account. So I don't disgust her! Shame disappears as if by magic, is replaced by excitement. What happiness! My hand leaves the breast on which it has been resting and descends to Suzanne's stomach, while my whole body once again moves in time with hers. I can wait no longer. I can't dawdle any longer. My finger slides into Suzanne's fleece.

This time no more exaltation but a veritable delirium: Suzanne explodes under my hand with frantic thrusts, opens up in a series of deep rhythmic waves. I lick her, lap at her shoulder-blade. I have the impression I'm drowning in her, drinking her in, devouring her whole. My clutching hand can go no further forward or back, rubbing, exploring, returning, sinking in deep, pulling out. I can't stop myself any longer.

I'll never stop. Together we no longer dive, we fly, we skim. I'm your man, my woman. I'm your prick my little cunt, my little slave. I'm muttering anything that comes into my head, I don't know what I'm saying, words I didn't know I knew. Faster, faster finger, quick prick, fast shaft, speed machine, faster Suzanne, marvellous, my cock on your clit, wank wank, keep going . . .

And then with no transition, I'm calm. I give her orders: on your back, don't move, spread your thighs. There, my motion slows. Stops, even, since I sense she's about to come. She quivers in a way I recognize, when all of a sudden there's no controlling will or desire, just the body being swept away and forgetting why.

She groans with disappointment. I smile and console her. My Suzanne . . . I must calm down even more, for I don't know why but I'm absolutely determined not to come, anyhow. I've the impression that all I'd take for myself I'd be stealing from her.

I don't know how much time passes before I manage to bring her close to me again. If her desire was thwarted, so was mine, at several points. She pulls away irritably, yet all the same she's too near now to forgo orgasm.

I get my bearings again, and this happens so often to me that here and now I excel myself. Her body is drenched with sweat. Her armpits are as liquid and hot as her sex. I plunge my nose, my tongue into them. Docile, she lifts her arms, folds them over my head. I let my lips and tongue move across her wet skin, adding my own sweat and saliva. The savage tang of her odour thickens with my own and I go down. My mouth reaches her fleece and I'm disgusted, fascinated. I know all too well how it will end. I don't want it to. I delay, hesitate. It's my turn to be dissatisfied.

She it is, finally, who, gripping my head between her hands forces it brutally down upon her sex, with an impatient and (I'd almost swear to this) angry gasp. I'll bite her, I'll cry. Yet the more disgust I feel, the more desire I have to be violent, to bite her, the gentler my tongue becomes, the more refined my kisses, the softer my lips become. Something tells me it's the only way to change my revulsion into love.

Suzanne's shriek is so violent, her orgasm so total and deep, that everything seems to resolve itself irrevocably, once and for all.

I'll never forget Suzanne's lovely exhausted face after her ecstasy. Thanks to her I have known early – and recognized always – the happy fragility of satisfaction achieved. She lies on her side, facing me. She is gently caressing my hair. She looks at me with amazement.

'You're so much stronger than I, Nea,' she tells me. 'I. have often wanted another girl. But I've never had the idea of trying anything.'

'Why not?'

'I don't know ... I used to think I was alone in experiencing certain desires ... And then ... how can I explain – I wouldn't have dared ... I haven't dared ...'

'Haven't you? But anyhow, you had the urge all right ...'

'Yes. Well, not exactly but ... It was years ago when I spent my holidays in Scotland as an au pair at Mary McGarrett's home. We got on well. She was going out with a guy and I had to chaperone her. Her parents were very strict Catholics. There was no question of her being on her own, not even for a few minutes. But we were all three allowed to go upstairs into Mary's room, where there was a piano. We were supposed to be singing old Scots ballads. Luckily for her, I'd play the piano. Immediately we were inside her room, they'd lie down together on Mary's bed. I'd play as loud as I could and we'd sing away more or less in unison.

'Need I say there were moments when I was the only one singing and believe me it wasn't always easy when I'd hear them sighing and gasping behind me. I just couldn't help myself, I had to turn round. Mary was only young, as was her boyfriend, whose name I forget – it was something like Jeremiah or Joshua, I don't know, one of those biblical names only the English, sorry the Scots, can dig up. The funny thing was, the boy didn't turn me on at all. He had a very pale white skin that was pink in places – something that doesn't attract me in the least. Mary, on the other hand, was absolutely beautiful, and what was more she enjoyed making love so much that it'd driven me to distraction myself. I belted out those Scots folksongs at the top of my voice, but in vain, for I could only think of her ...'

'But didn't you ever want to make love with them both?'

'No, not really, that was the sort of idea that never occurred to me ... But listen, Nea, it's incredible that you're asking me such questions.'

'What's incredible about it? It's no more incredible than your sleeping with Maurice.'

'That's not true, I don't sleep with him ... He really wants me to but I think it would be unwise of me.'

'Unwise, you say, but maybe it's because you don't really want to ...'

'Oh yes I do ... Well, I'm not very sure. I've made love with boys before. Doing it at home would worry me, though ... You know mother ...'

'I don't think it's because of mother. Are you sure Maurice loves you?'

'Of course he does ... Why would he be marrying me?'

'And what if he changed his mind?'

'If he changed his mind I certainly wouldn't cling on,' Suzanne replied, her tone rather sharp.

Just what I thought, it wasn't love. If someone were to ask me the same thing I'd answer: 'I'd fight tooth and nail.' I really think that things with Maurice and me will be a lot more honest. I look my sister in the eye: I'd like to make her explain herself. She doesn't really convince me ...

'I don't quite understand, Suzanne. Why didn't you say anything, to Mary at least?'

'You know Mary is Scottish and Catholic: well, although she did as she pleased and could send herself up quite amusingly, things like that just weren't mentioned. Besides, what could I have said to her?'

'That you too wanted to sleep with her.'

'Women don't sleep together. They . . .'

'Why not?'

'That'd be homosexuality.'

'What about what we've just done?'

'That's not the same, Nea . . . You're my sister . . . It's my fault, I shouldn't have. But I was half asleep and I didn't really know what I was doing either.'

'Did you like it?'

'Of course. But one mustn't do these things.'

'Why not, since we did. I've never heard you moan like that with Maurice.'

'I explained to you that Maurice and I have never really made love.'

'All the same, when he caresses you it does something to you. And don't you caress yourself when you're alone?'

'Listen Nea, you're impossible, asking such questions . . . Caress myself – what does that mean?'

'Well, I've been doing it since I was ten. One day quite by accident I started, because my nightie had ridden up against my snatch. I don't know how it happened. I rubbed a bit and then it was so nice I began again. I did it for almost a year with my nightie. But each time I had to get up and wash, as it got wet, so I preferred to do it with my finger and play with myself like that. Yes I often do it, every day, sometimes several times the same day. Don't tell me you don't . . .'

'Yes, but . . .'

'And when did you start playing with yourself? I look at you, Suzanne, and I get the impression you're a baby. All scared. Yet what I'm asking you isn't so complicated.'

'I was at least thirteen when I started . . .'

'Are you sure?'

'I think so. I don't remember. Anyway, one doesn't dwell on all that. But you're not corrupt, Nea. You always get such good reports . . .'

'I *don't* dwell on it the whole time. Anyway, I've too much work, what with school and everything else. There are plenty of other things I like. Honestly though, that's one of the nicest, isn't it?'

'No it is *not* one of the nicest things,' Suzanne replies, propping herself up on an elbow.

She adopts a stern look and continues:

'It's a childish habit, which has to stop some day. You'll have a man in your life, you'll love him and that's what matters.'

'Love is the most important thing, you're right.'

I'm in complete agreement with Suzanne. That's precisely why Maurice has made my whole past vanish at one fell swoop. I can't tell Suzanne yet. Maurice himself has to explain to her. Now she and I have made love she'll know very well that it's never been like that with her and Maurice. For me though, it's been that way with them both.

Basically there have been what are called great lovers. I was thinking of Juliet a moment ago, Juliet was a great lover. Great lovers are women more suited to love than others. Maybe I'm more capable of love than Suzanne. Or else – and this is likelier – she hasn't yet met the man she needs. Maurice too is mistaken. It's all absolutely clear: you can tell whether you love someone precisely by sleeping with them. In one sense I love Suzanne, love her now as I never did before.

'I think if you'd slept with Mary you'd have found out whether you really loved each other . . . Wouldn't it have been worth the risk?'

'To tell you the truth, I almost did,' Suzanne says quietly.

43

'I'll never forget it. I'd left her one evening when Jeremiah or Josh or whatever his name was had come to see her. They'd made love behind me while I tinkled on the piano, and I admit it affected me deeply. The boy had gone when I went to my room and undressed.

'I was half crazy. I told myself I'd go back into Mary's room and tell her I felt cold, tell her anything at all, but slide into bed beside her. Afterwards – we'd wait and see. I stood outside her door and was about to knock when I realized she'd already put out the light. Suddenly I didn't dare, I just stood rooted to the spot, shaking in my nightdress. I thought she might go to the bathroom and at that moment I might seize the opportunity to join her. But she didn't come out. Oh I stayed almost an hour. My heart was beating away but in the end I returned to my room . . .'

'Didn't you even play with yourself?'

'Yes . . . It wasn't the same.'

'Oh I know that all too well.'

I wonder whether to tell Suzanne everything. Her eyes need opening. But I realize also that it's nothing to do with me. She might think I've slept with her now in order to console her. Now that's not true, I slept with her because I love her, as much as Maurice. It's difficult to explain to people what one means by love. Luckily for Maurice, he's a man. He says things and does them, quite naturally. Though I'm small, thin, flat-chested, it didn't put him off. He loves me so much that none of that matters.

'You know, Suzanne, with Mary it was definitely love and you should have told her. I'm telling you, I know it's true – when you love someone, it's not at all difficult. You sleep together from the start. That's very important, since that way you're sure of each other. When you're sleeping together you get married if you want, or decide to live together, and that's it . . .'

'Well you do know a thing or two,' Suzanne smiles.

She jumps out of bed and grabs my hand.

44

'Come on, get back to your room, I must get dressed. Maurice'll be looking for me and I won't be ready ... So if I'm to take you at your word I ought to sleep with him tonight to find out if he loves me ...'

'Oh no, not with Maurice ... That'd be too late.'

'What do you mean, too late?'

How silly of me. It slipped out. But fundamentally it hasn't made things worse. When Maurice talks to her she'll remember what I've told her.

'You know, Suzanne, though you're learning, there's one thing you mustn't forget.'

'What's that?'

'I love you, darling.'

'Same here, idiot.'

'No Suzanne, not like that, I really do love you, love you like a man.'

'Like a man? You're my sister! It doesn't matter, though, I love you too, maybe not like a man, but I do.'

'As you like, but don't forget what I told you, Suzanne. Please don't ever forget.'

Chapter III

COLD HOLIDAYS

Perhaps it's an emptiness like the void
Yet so vast that Good and Evil together
Do not fill it.
Hate dies there of asphyxia,
And there the greatest love never penetrates.

Valéry Larbaud: *Poems by A. O. Barnabooth*

The holidays always make me lose my head. Going on holiday opens the floodgates to a torrent that submerges all. I who normally work so well find that what I like about holidays is the idea of nothing, really nothing to do.

Holidays mean disappearing in an out-of-the-way room or in a barn, going for endless solitary walks, or sitting with the old childhood favourites I've brought with me: serious or funny books, new or re-bound and repaired – *The Inn of the Sixth Happiness, Adventures of Marco Polo, Little Women*, or poetry books by Rimbaud and Verlaine.

The Christmas vacation is something else again. I have forgotten neither my books nor a good supply of those English boiled sweets I can find only in Paris. But what really makes me jump for joy–if I don't actually stop myself–is love. And love is something quite distinct from holidays. It's not simply an intense jubilation, it's the deep feeling of adventure and mystery which until now I've only recognized in some things I've read and of which I've had inklings. Love is the exploration of unknown territories. It's the delicious anguish of a happiness so unexpected, so undeserved that one fears losing it through ill-fortune, exactly as it came – by pure chance.

Maurice has married Suzanne. And there I was, briskly

46

closing their suitcases. My feelings haven't changed at all, however. On the contrary, they've grown stronger. I've matured. I understand: Maurice really loves me. That's why he has married my sister. After he had me, I was so happy I made a whole host of plans. I must have realized very quickly that they were unlikely, impossible even. You don't, for instance, need to be a fortune-teller to grasp the fact that mother and father wouldn't ever have let me marry just anyone. At a pinch, if I'd been pregnant ... if then.

I know my parents' theories. The subject came up one day during a meal. A young girl of sixteen, they were maintaining, isn't mature enough to be a mother. What would they have said to me? I'm not an utter fool. It's obvious that had Maurice declared point blank that we'd made love, he'd have been thrown out pretty smartly. So the only way for him to keep me was not to change the status quo and to marry my sister, to join the family and bide his time.

True, he should have spoken to me about it. I was a bit sulky with him, but he was so nice to me that I forgave him. He knows I love Suzanne too and he doesn't want to hurt her any more than I do. So there was no need to ask my permission when I would have given it him. I just think he should have told me once again straight out that I was his woman. He must be well aware that from now on there's no one else for me but him. Actually I think he humours me out of tact. Maybe he isn't quite sure of my love. So is he leaving me free to choose?

'I don't want to come on like a heavy father-figure, little Nea,' he said to me a few days after the wedding, 'but you and I have our work to be getting on with. You really must go on working like you've always done and pass your *baccalauréat*. As for me, I must make Suzanne happy. You love her too, don't you?'

'Of course I love Suzanne!'

'So you see,' he went on, 'we have the same problem to solve. And neither you nor I must deceive your parents.'

'That I do know. I know it all too well. If mother and father get wind of things, we're sunk.'

'I'm glad you understand.'

He looked extraordinarily relieved as he said those few words to me. And that's when everything became clear to me.

On the one hand he's ready to sacrifice himself for me, and that's why he hasn't told me again that he loves me and hasn't spoken of the future, but he's let me know that he loves Suzanne as I do, the same way I do, which is, basically, like a sister. And if he were so relieved, it's only because he's well aware that the least parental suspicion would be enough to separate us for ever – and he could no more stand that than I. I'm deeply grateful to him for the trust he has in me. *I've* doubted him: the reverse has never been true. I'd almost like to ask his forgiveness, but wouldn't that be behaving like a young girl again? No: like him I must simply wait; our reunion will only be the happier. Being a woman also means knowing when to keep silent. I'm going to show him he's not been mistaken.

I've kept silent, but it hasn't been easy. The wedding itself didn't present me with any problems. First of all I love weddings, and in a way this one was mine. The town hall, the church, the signatures – I found these reassuring. If the worst came to the worst and father or mother had suddenly found out what had happened between Maurice and myself, they'd just have had to like it or lump it. Maurice is their kinsman now. The lunch was delicious. I gorged myself, danced. A fat red-faced boy, a phoney type who'd been an old classmate of Suzanne's, kept dogging my footsteps. Obviously he was smitten. Maurice made me dance, too. Not once, but four or five times! He'd never talked to me this way before. He clasped me to him and told me all over again: 'Little Nea, now I know I can count on you. And you can rely on me too. You'll see . . .'

I think he'd drunk rather too much. I won't say he was drunk but he's generally reserved and he was talking a lot and louder than usual. Mother at one point treated him yet again in her 'commercial traveller' vein and he let her have some of her own medicine, calling her his 'mother-in-law'. I don't remember the exact comment but it was quite funny and mother turned her back on him, furious, but unable to accuse him of bad manners since he'd phrased his reply so neatly.

Suzanne and Maurice left at about six or seven p.m. I didn't even realize they'd gone. I was past caring. I was dancing with my fat admirer who was breathing down my neck and squeezing my left breast. I played with myself twice before going to sleep, thinking about Suzanne and Maurice. I felt like Dinarzade, Scheherazade's younger sister in *The Thousand and One Nights*. Each time I read the Mardrus translation of this book I imagine that at the end of each night, when it says: 'And King Schariar did with Scheherazade what he was wont to do', that Dinarzade (that'd be me) would faint with pleasure when after so many exciting stories the Commander of the Faithful made love to her sister.

On the other hand I found it harder to get used to Suzanne's being a wife. I hadn't realized just how much it would change our relationship. She and Maurice set up in an apartment very near ours – Rue Leonce-Papillard, a stone's throw from the Porte Maillot.

'You could say it'll almost be like being at home still,' mother said, 'but with all the advantages of independence.'

I never really grasped what this meant until I saw Suzanne busying herself with a host of household and kitchen equipment and knick-knacks. Otherwise she hasn't changed too much, she still lounges in bed for almost as long in the mornings, and it's mother who has to go to Saint-Pierre Market to find bits of material at bargain prices, mother who swaps gossip with the tradesmen.

Yet whether I like it or not, there's no place for me in their life. Suzanne did invite me to lunch. Once. We were rather awkward in each other's company and made small talk. It was never-ending. I took off, pretending I had some homework to do. Really I went to the cinema all on my own and I must confess I cried. No need to make a song and dance about it, but that meal had really done it: Suzanne had become a stranger and snobbish with it. Looking back, in one sense I was reassured. Maurice couldn't have been enjoying himself greatly either. Poor Suzanne. She's nice, but she's got no hidden depths or anything. And since Maurice no longer feels much for her physically, one wonders how he can stay with her.

I try my best to show Maurice I understand the situation. But it's not easy. I know he is right to play it safe, yet I wonder whether he isn't overdoing it just a little. It's practically impossible for me to find myself alone with him. The last time that happened, he said to me hastily:

'Nea, you know very well you promised me . . .'

'What did I promise you?'

'You know perfectly well. I'm married to Suzanne now. You must realize what that means.'

'Right, I do, but that doesn't change anything does it?'

'What are you talking about?'

'I'm only asking you, Maurice, if it changes anything. *I* haven't changed, I never will. You know what you told me, Maurice. I am a woman now. But one isn't a woman just for oneself alone. One is *somebody's* woman, a wife to a man.'

Maurice understood me very clearly but he looked bored. He must get it into his head, though, that this situation can't go on for ever. I too love Suzanne. We don't want to hurt her. Agreed. But we won't sort things out by delaying. Quite the opposite. It seems to me as if, in spite of everything, he still tends to treat me like a young girl. One would think it was telepathy, hearing him say:

'You're still only a kid, Nea,' as he places his hands upon my shoulders, looking me straight in the eyes. 'You have to put your future first, to think of yourself.'

'But you still love me, don't you?'

Now it's my turn to look him straight in the face. I'm not really worried, but from time to time I do need to hear him say it otherwise I couldn't go on.

'Of course I love you, my little Nea.'

He draws closer to me, puts his right arm around my shoulders and clasps me to him.

His thick tweed jacket scratches against my cheek. He is much taller than I. My head hardly comes up to his chest. I lower my eyes and look at his long legs, his feet. Suddenly I recall him stark naked, crushing me upon my bed and that thick sweater scratching me, his hand gripping me a bit too hard and making me hunch my shoulders – memories and hopes, past and present all merge, melt into a simple feeling of recognition: that's what a man is. Something harsh and very soft, a man whose woman I am . . . I raise my eyes and once again my glance meets his, he looks very distinguished.

'It's really true then, that you do love me like before and that you'll love me for ever?'

'Don't complicate matters, Nea.'

He starts laughing, a laugh I don't reckon is very natural but which I guess is to put me at ease.

'And how about you, do you still love me?'

'You know I do.'

'So if you still love me, cheer up. I like little Nea to be cheerful. Don't forget, in less than a week we'll all be together in the chalet. You, and Suzanne too – we mustn't forget Suzanne now, must we? All together at the chalet for the holidays. You still appreciate those kinds of holidays, when everyone's reunited ... Don't you think that for the moment that's the best answer I can give you?'

Of course it's the best answer. This holiday we're going to spend together is the first step. But I think it's an opportunity also, since we'll all be very close and we can clear matters up. Suzanne loves me too, and after all, we've shared something as sweet and almost as strong ... Anyway, she'll keep us, Maurice and myself. We're not going to abandon her because we love each other. Maurice need only tell the truth. He'll be the first to feel better for it, I'm sure of that. To begin with, it really isn't necessary to let our parents in on the secret. They certainly wouldn't understand. On the other hand, everything between the three of us will be simplified. One won't need to cover up any more. Maurice will obviously be much happier, and who knows, perhaps we'll open Suzanne's eyes, not only where she herself is concerned – she'll immediately see the difference between Maurice's feeling for me and the wretched travesty of love they enact with one another – but above all, realizing it's a genuine love, she in her turn will prepare herself for the person fate has in store for her. I repeat under my breath 'the person fate has in store for her'. I like this expression a lot. Perhaps I read it somewhere. That, I tell myself happily, is a real woman's thought. I am a woman. Maurice said so, not I. He didn't only say so, he proved it: I *am* a woman. That's exactly why Maurice chose me, because I am a woman. And today if I skip shamelessly like a little girl when I think about the Christmas holidays, that's because I'm finally sure, will prove it again once and for all, prove to the man I love that he wasn't mistaken, that I'm his woman for ever.

Our chalet is at Gruyère, very near the small village of Charmey. It's a large wooden farmhouse decorated with hunting trophies nailed to the south front. For all its size, it gives me a feeling of security: it's comprised of many niches and tiny wooden rooms in which one feels protected. Everything is honey-coloured: the walls of varnished logs, the pine partitions, steps and staircases, the vast kitchen table, the great chimney, the benches, footstools and rocking chairs by the hearth.

As ever, mother has added her personal touch, scattering colourful cushions everywhere to match the delicate, old-fashioned curtains. A widow, Mme Mortier and her daughter Jeannette live in a little annexe and look after the chalet all the year round. We can arrive without notice: in a few minutes, with that inimitable resinous odour of the traditional Gruyère farmhouses, fires will be blazing in the big fireplace of the main room and in the other rooms too. On arrival, I always experience the same keen pleasure on seeing in the distance, outlined against the blue December sky, the roof covered in snow which thickly overhangs the façade and north side of the chalet, and its tiles made out of overlapping little scales of light wood like the side of some huge blond whale.

Maurice and Suzanne are walking ahead of me and I'm watching them with a cheerful tenderness. I stoop, plunge my hands into the snow and pelt them with big snowballs that burst over their fur hats. They turn round and bombard me back. Jean-Marc, a distant cousin slightly younger than I, whom mother regularly invites for Easter and Christmas, joins in the battle, but suddenly I lose interest and tell him to stop. Like all boys his age he is incapable of knowing when to stop, and goes on hurling snowballs that explode over my neck and splatter into tiny freezing trickles down my back. I am furious and have a row with him. Maurice and Suzanne have the greatest difficulty calming me down. But we go into our rooms and I soon forget my fleeting ill-humour in a nice hot bath. When I go down to the main room, everyone's already there drinking wine.

The Pamprenier couple, a childhood friend of mother's

and her husband, a lawyer from the Midi, have come with us, as they do every year. As has old Mademoiselle Etchevery, a Basque lady who helped father during the war, so he could escape into Spain. Finally, there's Jean-Marc, who exasperates me, though I must admit he is better-looking than most boys of his age. He's quite tall, with curly black hair, big chestnut-brown eyes and ever such long lashes. From that point of view, he's OK, not even a pimple on his smooth skin. But he's not very smart. He loves tennis and is very proud of his skiing. He's won badges since he was seven. I'm rather good at skiing, but I couldn't care less about all that, and when he starts telling me about his feats and extolling Val d'Isère at the expense of Charmey, I tell him where to get off. I don't give a damn about the slopes at Val d'Isère and I'm just as happy skiing unpretentiously among the German Swiss and petty bourgeois French who come to this unassuming little place. If on the other hand I try talking to him about a book I like, he's out of his depth at once and answers me with stock phrases. My only pleasure where he's concerned is pulling his leg and ordering him about. The moment we really talk together, I make my arrangements.

'Come to my room at midnight tonight, I've something to talk to you about.'

'Midnight? But your parents won't let us do that!'

'Of course they wouldn't, usually, but they and the other guests don't arrive till next week, New Year's Eve. So we'll be alone for six days, and I intend to take advantage of that.'

'Don't you think that Suzanne . . .'

'Oh Suzanne can mind her own business! She's not going to play the heavy mother just because she's got married. And you'll do as I say.'

Jean-Marc knocks on my door punctually at midnight. I can't exactly explain why, but in my mind this visit is linked with the story Suzanne told me about her stay with Mary McGarrett. I keep Jean-Marc waiting quite a while. He knocks a second time and I still don't budge. He must have seen the light under my door but doesn't dare make a sound, for fear of waking the others. Yet he doesn't go away. I'm not sure how long I make him wait. I'm imagining Suzanne, grown-up Suzanne, my darling Suzanne not daring to enter Mary's room. It's rather as if I want to punish Jean-Marc by making him relive the same experience as Suzanne. But when I realize he's about to leave – hearing his footsteps recede – I run and open up:

'Come on in quick,' I say to him under my breath. 'What are you doing? You know I've been waiting hours for you.'

'I . . . knocked twice.'

'Well, I must have been asleep. I was thinking about you, you know.'

It's amazing how ugly men's dressing-gowns and pyjamas are. He is looking really awkward in a sort of purple outfit that is all puckered above pyjama trousers of a striped material that have ridden up over his ankles.

'You do look odd!'

'If you're not pleased to see me, just say the word,' Jean-Marc complains sulkily.

I rather like him. He's got a nasty disposition. He flies off the handle for no reason at all, but he's kind and honestly there's something I like about him. I think perhaps it's the way he looks. People always say – at least teachers and certain sorts of adults do – that a boy or girl has an open face. I can't bear open faces. What's more, I know what the expression means. I've often studied my own in the mirror, and it couldn't be more open or honest. People respond favourably to it. Yet if they knew what I was really thinking! There's no reason why things should be different with others. Actually, people who always look you straight in the eye are always embarrassing: they usually end up doing the dirty on you. I far prefer someone who glances to the side or above or below or no matter where, so long as they don't stare at you like a curious animal. As for Jean-Marc, he has an intimate way of lowering his gaze. If he knew how sweet he is when he does that ... Luckily he doesn't have a clue – and *I* certainly won't tell him.

'Take off that frightful thing you're wearing.'

'My dressing-gown? What's the ...'

'It's vile. Horrid.'

'I suppose you think you're so marvellously turned out!' Jean-Marc retorted angrily.

'Better than you are, anyway!'

Still grumbling, he takes off his horrible dressing-gown. His pyjamas are hardly an improvement, but possibly because he looks very thin in them and very upset too, I feel I want to hug him. I'm not going to though. He'd be too happy, the idiot would spoil everything.

'Sit down in the armchair.'

'Why did you get me to come to your room?'

'Must I always tell you why I do things?'

'No, but I'm asking you, I just want to know why you wanted me to come here.'

'Didn't you want to?'

'You're really a pain, the way you always put people in the wrong! Yes, I'm glad. Are you satisfied? I'm happy I came, but tell me why you wanted me to. Surely that's not hard ...'

'I wanted to talk to you.'

'Well you *are* talking ...'

'What do you think of me?'

'*I* don't know.'

'Do you think I'm attractive or ugly?'

'Well for God's sake, what do you want me to say? Yes, you've got a very nice figure.'

'Would you like to see me naked?'

'You can be really aggravating sometimes ... What are you getting at?'

'This . . .'

This time I look him straight in the eye, not with an open look like the saying has it, but deep into his eyes so as to pin him down and prevent him from getting away. Since Maurice, I've become an observer. I know very well what's happening when men talking to me about this or that suddenly start staring or their voices sound strained for a split second . . . and then, hey presto, they carry on with the conversation, whatever its subject, seeming more assured than ever. You're supposed to believe they're innocent as lambs. It doesn't take me in any longer. Tonight Jean-Marc won't escape. He's not going to. I see at once that he's already a goner.

With one movement I pull my nightdress over my shoulders and head. It falls to the ground in a circle, like a faded rose. But I swear Jean-Marc isn't looking at that. He's staring at me, immobile and dumb.

'Happy?'

'Yes,' he murmurs.

His hands are gripping his knees so tightly that their knuckles have gone all white. He tries to get up.

'No, don't move, you mustn't. If you move, I'll get dressed again and you'll leave this room.'

'Nea . . .'

'Shut up, I don't want to listen to you. I'm the one who makes the decisions . . .'

I move away from him so that I'm standing almost in front of the full-length mirror just inside the bathroom door. I'm not looking at Jean-Marc now but at his reflection behind me and at my own. I spread my legs wider. With my left hand I caress my nipples in turn and they contract and harden. My right hand slowly descends along my stomach until it reaches my pubic hair and my finger lazily penetrates my sex. I've never before caressed myself standing up. Sometimes I've imagined it. Though it's been one of my favourite fantasies for some time I've never actually done it.

57

I've had other ideas and substituted other scenes for this one, but tonight memories of previous dreams return very clearly. Exactly how I'd always imagine myself standing in front of a man. Really it's far more difficult to arouse one-self standing up. I have to concentrate. I forget Jean-Marc momentarily. I need to close my eyes, for if I don't the pleasure doesn't last as long. My clitoris is dry: if I rub it too quickly and too hard, it'll just get sore to no purpose. I wet my finger with my tongue and rest it very gently on the tiny button of bliss. I scarcely revolve it, but vibrate it immedi-ately, and luckily everything slides into gear again. My vulva grows wetter, warms: I remember ... I return to a scenario familiar during the past few months, one within which I have come night after night, exhausting myself only to revive again, two or even three times in a row, before falling asleep overcome with pleasure and fatigue. I am walking on the lawn separating the Tuileries gardens from the arch at the Place du Carrousel. I am looking at all the statues of naked women, one by one, and the desire for climax rises in me as if each of the statues had just taken its pleasure right before my eyes. My buttocks and breasts grow rounder, fuller, I become heavier, and I am walking with more and more difficulty. Then I reach an empty pedestal, a narrow plinth on to which I climb, and there, with a few almost imperceptible gestures, I shed my clothes. I've nothing to unbutton or unhook. They fall from me of their own accord (just like my nightdress); they leave me like petals, like a wind-driven cloud, and with no difficulty at all I assume a wonderfully comfortable posture, as if my hips are sustained by the air itself. The passers-by notice nothing. They do not know I am a real woman; in their eyes I am just a statue like the others – until the moment when one of them does notice me, and stops in front of me, also shedding his clothes, like a snake sloughing off its skin. He appears before me nude, but not nude like the men I've so far seen naked: he is perfectly proportioned, built exactly like those Greek statues from my

Art History classes, with a slight bulge of the buttocks and a small compact cock, tight-furled, with a curly and dense fleece. He stops, looks at me, places his hand like a shell over his cock which I can no longer see, and at that moment my own hand closes upon my bush, my finger sliding imperceptibly into the valley of my vagina. I bear down a bit harder, turn a little quicker, and ecstasy floods me just as the man facing me takes away his hand and discovers instead of a prick there, an animal, a sort of weasel or otter with pointed muzzle, sparkling eyes, and thick brown shiny fur gleaming like silk. With the self-same motion, man and beast leap upon me and my belly is devoured by a living, burning mouth: male caresses, animal bites, I don't know which. I open my eyes, groaning, and in answer to my groan comes Jean-Marc's: he is lolling in his armchair, his erect prick in his right hand. Suddenly myself again, I tell him: 'No, stop!'

Jean-Marc, half-surprised, obeys, looking at me strangely. A fearful, submissive, passive kind of look. Which Jean-Marc has to pay for, such is my edgy mood.

'Sorry Nea . . . I don't know what got into me . . .'

'Don't be silly, Jean-Marc, you saw me come and you want to come too. Dead simple, I'll help you.'

'Do you love me?' Jean-Marc asks in a toneless voice.

'Of course not.'

Ignoring my reply, Jean-Marc gets up and moves towards me with his arms outstretched. Obviously he wants to kiss me. He's absolutely ridiculous with his pyjama pants fallen round his ankles and his top pulled up to disclose his still stiff prick and thighs and calves that are far too thin.

'Take off your pyjama top and sit down again.'

'I love you Nea, you know . . .'

'Don't say such stupid things, you got excited watching me come. That's normal, but I warn you, don't try and touch me, still less kiss me – or else you'll find yourself back on the landing before you know what hit you.'

Jean-Marc hardly knows where he is any more, and once again this pleases me. He's definitely rather sweet. Especially now he's naked. Even his thinness makes him appealing. Every time I talk to him his penis inflates, hardens, grows longer. As if playing a music all its own. I'm delighted. I approach him and stand behind his armchair. He can't see me. I softly stroke his shoulders and then his arms. When my hands are close to his he tries to grip them. At this point I stop him yet again: 'I told you not to do anything unless I asked you to. Keep your hands to yourself.'

I continue my caresses .. My hands glide over his stomach, carefully avoiding prick, thighs, knees. He leans forward, trembling like a leaf, and sighs, making odd little gasps. I like all this enormously. I go on in the same way for some minutes and then I take hold of his penis in my right hand. With the left I gently caress his lips, half-open them, slide my fingers one by one into his mouth as if they were tiny male organs penetrating dolls. That's another picture I like. I rock forward, thinking of this sort of miniaturized love. But he can hardly bear it any longer. Suddenly I too have had enough. Must finish. I speed up my caresses. Everything is happening very fast. He tenses convulsively, accelerates the tempo, and I also go faster and faster: he's disgusting me, boring me. I want to get it over and done with – and I finish things off. He spurts, covering his torso and the arms of the chair with sperm. I feel a sudden spasm of tenderness and would like to hold him next to my heart and tell him lots of very tender and gentle things, but almost immediately the sight of the sperm, the whitish smears across his goosey skin and on the chair, irritate me and I confine myself to saying dryly to him: 'Get up and clean yourself up, especially the stains you've made all over the chair! I warn you, next time that's your problem. Those stains are hard to get rid of – and they're revolting.'

'Right,' Jean-Marc says meekly.

He gets up, goes to the bathroom and cleans up.

'Don't use my towel . . There's some Kleenex in the bathroom cupboard . . .'

He comes back into the room, dresses and once again approaches me as if intending to kiss me.

'No, I've already told you, that's out of the question.'

'As you like, Nea. Good night.'

'Good night.'

Without moving or putting anything on I watch him leave. He shuts the door behind him. I swear to myself that it's the last time I'll do that.

The next day, though, I do it again, and the day after that too.

Whenever he sees me now, Jean-Marc has a hangdog expression. I can't help making sarcastic digs at his expense, mocking him in company, humiliating him in any way that occurs to me. It's become the standing joke of these holidays.

'Where's your scapegoat then?'

'What's poor Jean-Marc done to you?'

'Leave Jean-Marc alone . . .'

'Jean-Marc, when are you going to put this little snob in her place?'

Sometimes it all amuses me and at other times my heart is filled with regret, but I can't help it, there it is.

Fortunately Christmas at the chalet reunites us all under an avalanche of traditions and laughter that each year sweeps us away without leaving us time to breathe or brood over our petty problems.

It's Maurice's first time here, and at the beginning he has a bit of difficulty adapting. This particular week there's no more privacy. Everyone goes in and out of each other's rooms quite freely, and breakfast or drinks are consumed here, there and everywhere – on the edge of a bed, at the huge table in the main hall, and in father's little library, normally sacrosanct and out of bounds when he's here. We eat like pigs, ski like lunatics, sleep like logs.

Suzanne's suntan rivals new-baked bread. She is so lovely she should be crowned Queen of Charmey, queen of our chalet. I mention this to her and she tells me kindly that I'm crazy. I don't know why, but ever since we arrived here she's been very concerned about me.

On the twenty-fourth we discuss going to midnight mass, then abandon the idea. It's finally decided that we'll have an early night and open our presents next morning over one of those enormous breakfasts of cold meats, cheese, black bread, white bread, home-made bread, rolls and the rest, which, says Maurice, are the charm of Charmey.

Jean-Marc finds these pathetic puns and family in-jokes all a bit much. One can't blame him. And I don't do much to make him feel at ease. He's rather confused by the way I perpetually blow hot and cold where he is concerned: caresses yes, kisses no, pleasure certainly but no affection. He doesn't really understand what's going on and neither do I.

Is it my fault if I don't honestly want to see Christmas in with him, and Suzanne brings me my nicest present by coming to kiss me in bed? Kissing me just as we kissed before ... As if wanting to strengthen our bond. She rocks me softly, soothes sorrows I don't even have, overwhelms me with love. Huddled together under the duvet, we temporarily forget Maurice altogether.

He it is who won't be forgotten and comes to reprimand Suzanne and tease me: but he kisses me gently, letting me know it's bedtime.

I watch the two of them go, she putting her arm around him and resting her head on his shoulder, then leaving him suddenly at the door to run to my bed and kiss me again: 'Happy Christmas, darling Nea, Happy Christmas!'

She rejoins him but turns once again on the threshold before closing the door, as if wanting her final look of love to be directed at me. And I get a new insight: if I'm so sure of Maurice, it's because I am surer still of Suzanne. She'd never have been so available, so close to me had she belonged to him. In fact my certainty is twofold: it's because I love them both and they both love me that, obviously, there's nothing between them.

I recall this last week of December as being one long peal of laughter, like the sung laughter in operettas, full of trills and echoes, perhaps a little false but so expressive because of its very superficiality, that the whole auditorium cannot help sharing in it.

I've read in quick succession Balzac's *The girl with the golden eyes*, Margaret Kennedy's *The Constant Nymph*, *Diloy the Railwayman* by the Countess de Ségur, and *Lords of the Instrumentality*, an SF novel by an American whose name I forget. In two afternoons I've got through all my holiday set texts. I've written a letter to Mademoiselle Mullet, our Latin teacher who's leaving the *lycée* because of ill health. She's always been very nice to me and it's really thanks to her that I'm top. All this hasn't stopped my skiing for four hours each morning and beating Jean-Marc every time by a good three minutes down the slopes. Some days I get the idea I could still be fitting in much else also, but I'm not sure what. I do like adding up all the moments that make up a day. But whenever I have a moment I think about Maurice and Suzanne. Now they merge together in my mind: when I play with myself in front of Jean-Marc, I think of Maurice; I think of him still when I'm caressing Jean-Marc, but I'll be talking to Jean-Marc about Suzanne. It always happens the same way: I sit him down in the big chintz-covered armchair in my bedroom, quite naked. I position myself behind him, caress his shoulders, chest, stomach, and descend towards his penis while describing Suzanne in detail. Each evening I invent a new scene, either with Suzanne already nude so that I strip for him, or with Suzanne coming up close to me, lying alongside my body, with me stroking her. I sometimes masturbate Jean-Marc four or five times running. Naturally I haven't told him I'm offering him Suzanne. It's none of his business, but it is *her* body, her eyes, hands, all her gestures – indeed the way she responds to caresses and the way she caressed me – that I'm giving him. I'm literally gorged with pleasure. I almost reach the point where I'm sickened by it, as if I'd eaten too many cream cakes in a patisserie. I must admit it's Jean-Marc who gets the worst of it at these moments. I'm hateful to him. I know it but can't help myself, he annoys me with that whining manner of his. If he doesn't like the situation, well, no one's forcing him to come to my room. *I* shan't go looking for him in his room if one night he doesn't come to mine.

This morning I find it hard to believe it's still only the twenty-eighth of December. The time is certainly passing very quickly, but the days are so full that each of them is never-ending, like those serials of long ago by Xavier de Montepin or Ponson du Terrail which I've found in the chalet library. I've had time to take off in my ski gear and we've climbed up to Vounetz and spent three pleasant hours there.

Arriving back at the chalet at suppertime I am worn out and famished. We make ourselves a huge ham omelette as lunch and tea combined. Then we all watch an old film on TV and eat dinner. Jean-Marc begins gazing ecstatically at me. I tell him I'm feeling shattered and don't want to see him later. His face falls. I don't give a damn as I'm feeling in a good humour.

After dinner Maurice begins a poker game with the Pampreniers and the Jauffreys, utterly uninteresting neighbours we've always seen in the past just because they too come to Charmey most holidays.

I climb up to my room and get things organized for a

voluptuous evening: a long bath in herb-scented oil pinched from mother, who has forbidden me to use it on the grounds that it's too expensive. I put on my little nightie embroidered with lilies, which father gave me last year as a New Year gift. I chuck three cushions on to my bed, switch the TV channel to a repeat showing of a Bob Dylan concert, open a bar of milk chocolate and stack up a pile of paperbacks to choose from when I feel like it: an old Black Mask detective novel, *Doctor Fu Manchu* by Sax Rohmer; the third volume of the Jalna trilogy (I've read the first two) and a mass of Lucky Luke comics. Finally I flip through the comics and the Fu Manchu.

It must be around one a.m. There are no TV programmes on any more, and I'm peckish. I get ready to go down to the kitchen in my dressing gown; but at the top of the stairs I hear voices. It's odd, for usually everyone's asleep by eleven. As I'm not feeling sociable and don't want any remarks made about my projected raid on the larder, I creep on tiptoe to the bottom of the staircase so I can see who's there.

All the lights are out except for one Japanese lantern in a corner. The fire in the big chimney lights the main room, and in its glow I can see Suzanne and Maurice lying on the enormous white bearskin on the hearth. They've taken a big cushion. Maurice is on his back and Suzanne is lying against him, in profile, her head resting on his shoulder. As they often do in the evenings, they're both wearing djellabas: Maurice's is a fine white woollen one and Suzanne's is blue silk, embroidered with multicoloured flowers. They make a splendid couple. I long to run down there and embrace them both but, stupid though it may seem, I'm shy and stay rooted to the spot, not daring to descend or even return to bed, for fear of making a noise on the parquet.

From where I am, however, I can hear their voices whispering as clearly as if I were beside them.

'I promise you this is the last year, darling.'

Suzanne has just stammered out these words. Leaning

forward I can see her hand slip inside the neck of Maurice's djellaba.

'Believe me,' says Maurice, leaning up on one elbow, 'I like them all. And these family gatherings are very enjoyable, but I'd rather we were alone on such occasions. I work all year round, I go rushing here and there on my trips, I take off for two days to Beziers and have three in London, and don't ever get back home even for lunch. Well, I'd like to, but at least we ought to be together, especially during holidays like this . . .'

'I understand,' Suzanne replies, 'but you know what mother and father are like, particularly mother. You know she doesn't like you. Our marriage didn't exactly thrill her. So we can easily make one or two minor allowances . . . And then there's Nea.'

'Nea's a kid.'

'She's my sister . . . We *have* always lived together. She needs me.'

'That remains to be seen!' Maurice says. 'You're under some illusions about Nea. There's a little madam who's quite able to look after herself.'

What a tone! How can Maurice talk about me in this way? It's understandable that he wants to hide his feelings from Suzanne, but still, to talk about me so coldly, as if I were a stranger, a nuisance even. A shudder runs through me.

'You know Nea seems to be a sensible girl. True, she is an excellent student. But you can't imagine how sensitive she is . . .'

'Right, let's discuss just how sensitive!' says Maurice. '*I* think she reads far too much. It gives her all sorts of precocious ideas. I don't think your parents are strict enough with her. I'm wondering whether it mightn't do her good to go to boarding school . . . That way you wouldn't be playing the elder sister role any longer . . .'

What's the matter with him? Is this Maurice who's talking of sending me away? The one who hardly three months ago was calling me his wife. The one who showed me he loved me, who took my virginity . . . Virginity. I feel a sob in my throat, and I suppress it, half-choking. I all but cough.

'Enough of Nea . . . Don't you think?' Suzanne protests, her voice sharper.

While uttering these last words her hand has moved to the shoulder of Maurice's djellaba, which she's pulling up. Maurice half turns to make it easier for her. Then he sits up and takes it off. He leans forward and in turn undresses Suzanne. They are both naked.

'You're quite crazy,' Suzanne says with a faint smile. 'You realize anyone could open a door and see us . . .'

'So what, we're married aren't we? I've always dreamed of making love in front of a log fire.'

'You're reckless . . . my love . . .'

Maurice is lying upon Suzanne. He is caressing her breasts. His hand moves downward along her thighs and legs, which part spontaneously.

I've so often caressed myself while thinking about them making love, but now I feel a chill envelop me. Not only does it not excite me, but I'm overwhelmed by a kind of panic. However, it's still impossible not to look.

'Careful! You're hurting me,' Suzanne complains.

'Sorry . . . I'll put it in as gently as possible, I promise,' says Maurice.

He's on top of her and I see their bodies slowly writhing. Suzanne sighs in the way I know so well. It's Maurice's breathing I recognize above all, a sort of gasp I've remembered. I can tell almost to the second how his gasps will quicken. And they do accelerate, just as I expect.

'That's good.'

'I'm not hurting you?'

'No no, Maurice. Just the opposite. Put it in deeper, harder. Further in . . . Fuck me till it sticks out of my throat. Split me open . . . Deeper.'

67

'Do you love me, Suzanne?'

'You know I do,' Suzanne whispers. 'Do *you*?'

Maurice doesn't immediately reply. His breathing starts to wheeze. His sighs get louder, harsher, become raucous.

'Suzanne, my Suzanne . . . My wife . . . wonderful, Suzanne . . . you're marvellous . . . you're my woman, my wife . . . marvellous, wonderful . . . my woman . . .'

Liar! He said all of that, wife, woman, wonderful marvellous – just the same way, in exactly the same tone, the same faltering tone of voice – when he said it to me. The liar, I won't wait for him. I'll never ever wait any longer. I rise to my feet and head for my room, not even bothering about the noise I might be making. They've got other things on their minds, both of them. The liars! What sort of game is Suzanne playing? My own sister! Why did she come and kiss me in my room? Why did she pretend I was someone special to her? As for him, he tricked me. Mother was right. She's never trusted him, and I thought she was being suspicious and unfair. She was quite right . . . What a cheat! How unfair! What can I do? I'm his wife – Maurice told me so. Even if he did tell Suzanne, too. It just proves he's a liar. I'm his wife. You don't have two wives. *I* am his wife.

Chapter IV

SETTING THE SCENE

What is a major battle? It is a major physical struggle, not an insignificant skirmish to attain a secondary objective.

Karl von Clausewitz: *On War*

I don't see why Maurice should get away with it just because he's a grown man. *I* didn't make him assure me I was a woman. If he thinks he can change his mind at will, he's mistaken. I'm not going to let him calmly pack me off to boarding school while he and Suzanne make fun of me.

They're all just the same, Maurice, mother, father: they think we know nothing about love or life's obscenities ... Flashers, for instance. I knew all about them when I was half the age I am now – which was when I first saw one. I never said anything about it to my parents or anyone else. There were three or four of us at the little *lycée* when I was still in the junior form who'd have some laughs whenever we spotted old Father Pipi. We'd call him that among ourselves because as soon as he saw us he would open his flies and grin at us. We would laugh at him and run away and pretend to be scared though actually we weren't at all. I must say I even thought him rather nice. And I was quite content to see him with his trousers undone. It made me feel like scratching myself, made me want to stretch my limbs and laugh, and so I used to laugh louder than the others. One day we didn't see him again, and we heard he'd been arrested. I also knew that people who asked small children to follow them got arrested. Unfortunately nobody ever offered me sweeties! I think I'd have accepted precisely because it was forbidden. I've always known that where I'm concerned that sort of person or situation doesn't turn out to be dangerous.

I learned of the existence of rape through the newspapers. When a man sleeps with a woman who doesn't want to, it's rape and he's sent to prison. There: no need to look any further.

If I want him to, Maurice will go to prison. *He's* the one who wants to send me to boarding school. When he sees that *I* can send him to prison he'll think twice about that. It's not difficult, I'll say he raped me, and just when they're about to send him to prison I'll explain that it's not true. He'll be grateful to me for having saved him, he'll thank me tearfully. We'll all go back home together and that's when I'll inform my parents that I've agreed to live with him and Suzanne. We'll all work out a way of arranging things. Soon maybe we can love each other without hiding the fact. As for Suzanne, I'm sure she'll be only too willing.

I said that I knew what rape was. I realize now that that's not strictly true. How exactly does it happen? What is necessary to make it rape? I see that if I make a mistake, they'll know it's not true. And this time I'd finish up at boarding school as Maurice proposes. I'd be treated like a liar and punished. No, that won't do. I really must find out in detail everything there is to know about rape.

Thanks to Mademoiselle Etchevery I should be able to do that without too much trouble. For two days the weather has been awful. The Pampreniers play bridge endlessly and the elderly, rather puritanical spinster, who thinks children ought to live in the open air, doesn't really like to see me hanging around the chalet. She sits in a rocking chair in the chimney corner, reading prewar British detective novels in Tauchnitz editions. The chalet is full of them. I think my grandfather collected them.

In her thick black and white tweed suit she herself has the air of an Agatha Christie heroine. When I approach her she stares at me over her spectacles and says gruffly: 'For heaven's sake don't tell me you're at a loose end. At your age one never is . . .'

'Not at all, Mademoiselle,' I reply brightly. 'Quite the opposite. I've decided to take the opportunity of getting ahead with my set work, and I need you . . . I don't like to ask, but I have to get to the main library at Fribourg for some books I need. Could you possibly drive me in in father's old car, the Renault 4 he leaves here at the chalet? I know he wouldn't mind . . .'

'Well, if you promise to go for a good long healthy walk first . . . Two hours before lunch – all right?'

'Oh, *thank* you, Mademoiselle!'

The fresh air is really rather pleasant after all. The wind chaps my cheeks and my ears ache, yet my whole body is warm: my hands are deep inside my mittens, my feet in their lined bootees. And while walking I can work out my plan. I'm on top of the world.

At lunch I'm absolutely ravenous. I eat enough for four people and Mademoiselle Etchevery congratulates me.

The last mouthful of dessert swallowed, we hop into the Renault and are in the Fribourg library by three p.m. There's no one in the reading room, perhaps because of the holidays. Mademoiselle Etchevery talks for a few minutes to the librarian, a fat simpering biddy who bends over backwards to be of service to us French ladies. After introducing us, Mademoiselle Etchevery tells me she'll come back to collect me at five thirty, then she takes off.

Now I'm faced with an unforeseen problem. There are a certain number of books one can borrow without filling in a reservation form: dictionaries, history books, atlases, even a medical encyclopaedia. Right, so much for the latter: I rifle through it but find nothing really interesting under *Rape* except a list of book titles, notably a *Treatise on Forensic*

Medicine by Professor Karl Mulstein. Yet if I'm to make a request for this I'm afraid the librarian may ask questions.

It's idiotic. Try as I may, I can't see a way round the difficulty. But this must be my lucky day. The librarian summons an old white-moustached assistant, some sort of caretaker or attendant. She whispers a few words to him and he nods. She gets up, puts on her coat and gloves, dons a hat adorned with a pheasant feather that cleaves the air like a sword, and disappears through the baize entrance door.

The old fellow takes her place. I hesitate no longer and slip him a form he doesn't even read. He confines himself to repeating the reference number loudly and, shuffling along, vanishes behind some shelves to reappear moments later, presenting me with a large volume completely re-bound in black cloth.

I return to my place, but after an hour I have to admit I've made scarcely any progress. I've only copied a single paragraph into my notebook and it still mystifies me somewhat: 'If the penis has remained outside the hymen itself, this constitutes in medical jurisprudence indecent assault, i.e. a misdemeanour punishable by imprisonment without remission or suspension of sentence. Should penetration have been completed *ultra hymene*, a criminal offence has been committed carrying with it a penalty of imprisonment with hard labour.'

I know all about hymens but I don't understand much else of this. Anyway, I can't get any practical help from the above. Luckily, once again there's a bibliography which solves the dilemma. From it I locate a title which should provide me with the guidelines I need: *Society and Sexual Repression* – Ten Years of Criminal Law and Morality in the Canton of Basle.

I wasn't mistaken. Just like the first time, the assistant gave me the book I asked for, only examining the reference number. I had a narrow escape there, for the librarian returned a minute or so after I'd obtained it. I'm reading detailed case histories of various rapes, illustrations included on facing pages. One of them particularly strikes me. It's the case of quite an old man, aged about fifty, arrested for interfering with twelve year old girls. He lived in the same block of flats, and on the school half holidays he would contrive to lure them into his apartment, naturally offering them sweets and showing them pictures. These pictures, the book states, were of a special kind: no further details are given. After which he would make them undress and they'd play together, looking, touching each other, cuddling. Then he would send them home, showering them with presents – dolls, balloons, sets of toys. The little girls liked him a lot and never said anything to their parents. It was the concierge, entering the apartment unexpectedly when the old man had forgotten to lock the landing door, who surprised them. She informed the parents and called the police. The little girls cried bitterly when the man they called their 'Best Friend Bruin' was arrested. He had nicknamed them his two little honey bees. When the police commissioner consoled them, saying that the nasty man wouldn't bother them any more, they cried even more, blurting out that he wasn't nasty and they wanted to see him again there and then. The author comments at length on 'this grave case of corruption of suggestible minors.'

It takes me ages to understand what all this business is about. To begin with, it moves me more than I can express. I stop reading: my heart pounding, my eyes shut, and oddly enough I see Old Father Pipi's image. It's him and yet it's not – rather as though he's been transfigured. His hair, instead of being dirty grey is a lovely shining silver. His white wrinkled face glows like those in religious paintings. His overcoat has turned into a lovely flowing dressing-gown rather like father's beige vicuna one, all warm and soft. I see him standing in a room like the one where the old man invited the little girls; he walks across, opens the door for me, and I enter, somewhat shyly. He kindly asks me to sit down and I obey him as he walks up and down in front of me. He has a nice gentle smile. He asks me to lift my skirt and I do so; to take off my knickers, which I also immediately do. He undoes his dressing-gown cord. He has a long, very white body, the skin is a little wrinkled. He is thin rather than muscular, but I keep noticing that the texture of his skin is white, and quite strong although it seems fragile. He begins by whispering that I can play with myself if I wish . . .

At this I open my eyes. I can't wait. I leave my seat and go to the library toilets where I lock myself in. My back leaning against the wall, cheeks scarlet, stomach muscles rigidly tensed, I close my eyes once again.

'. . . yes, play with yourself,' the silver-haired man continues.

Gently I place my finger between the lips of my vagina. The little girl of my dream lowers her eyes and stares at the floor. I close mine tighter so I can imagine still more. I purse my mouth and grind my teeth as if I were eating a lemon. My other hand, the left, rests on my thigh and I stroke myself softly from knee to buttock – that is, the man with the silver hair approaches, leans forward and caresses me with his old, very clean soft hand, while his thick member, solid and brownish, bobs gently against my cheek and my left hand seizes his swollen organ while I rub myself faster. I open my mouth, I want to swallow this marvellous brown member but I can't, it's too large, my mouth is too small, so I stick out my tongue and it glides very gently over skin downy as a peach.

'You see, when I was quite young,' the silver-haired man goes on. 'I used to dream that one night my Aunt Claire would come into my room and open her nightgown as I've just done for you, and she would be as near me as I am to you and rub her stomach and bush over my face just like I've stroked your cheek with my cock, and that when her bush tickled my lips I'd come, just like this . . .'

74

It bursts from him, all milky and warm like Jean-Marc's, but far more powerfully and plentifully. Under his hand I have the sensation that my whole womb has exploded also, that it's molten, blazing, volcanic ...

I return to my seat and carefully copy out the passages that interest me. I can't use the story of the old man and the two small girls. That just interested me personally. It's done something to me, something important, the significance of which I'll discover later: for the time being I'll take down every detail that might help me. I'm calm now and very content. Everything is working out well and I've all I need. When Mademoiselle Etchevery arrives I fling my arms around her neck.

'My essay'll be great!'

'You're always the same!' exclaims Mademoiselle Etchevery, pushing me off and laughing.

She can't bear gushing behaviour.

'You're the only girl I've ever seen get through homework like cream cakes,' she adds, affectionately patting my cheek.

I sense her admiration and it delights me. In the car we chatter away like starlings.

'We had a very good time,' she declares to the Pampreniers, subsiding into an armchair, all breathless, instead of sitting as she usually does, very rigidly in an upright chair.

I stare at her long bony pinched features. It's silly, but I can't help liking Mademoiselle Etchevery.

I haven't allowed Jean-Marc into my room for two days now. He's given up skiing and does all he can to get me alone with him, but I have no difficulty outwitting him and his rather obvious ruses. I'm sure he's been crying on his own. His eyes are puffy and red. Still, he'll get over it.

Today's the day: the thirtieth of December, when my parents arrive, the day Maurice will discover what young girls are capable of, the day on which, for starters, I'll console Jean-Marc.

I have no trouble at all there. I stay in bed the entire morning as the weather's horrible, all leaden and overcast, so that the roofs of the neighbouring chalets are hardly visible and the valley is shrouded in a yellowish mist. We're so gloomy that Suzanne decides to make a big cheese fondue for lunch, even though it's really a dinner dish, just to cheer everybody up. While the Pampreniers and Mademoiselle Etchevery are having coffee I challenge Jean-Marc, Maurice and Suzanne to Scrabble. Jean-Marc and myself team up. He thanks me with a big wet smile. We win, of course.

'Come on,' I say to him at the end of the game, 'I'll play you the latest Werewolves LP. Wait till you hear it, it's great, an American import. Father brought me back a copy last time he went to New York.'

Mademoiselle Etchevery climbs up to her room for a siesta. As for the Pampreniers and Maurice and Suzanne, nothing will tear them away from the endless game of bridge in which they're now engrossed.

'Why've you been avoiding me the last two days?' Jean-Marc complains plaintively.

'Am I avoiding you now? You're here aren't you, so what are you complaining about?'

'I'm not complaining,' Jean-Marc hastily explains, 'but I was wondering what you had against me . . .'

I shrug, begin to unbutton my tartan woollen shirt and take off my ski pants.

'What if somebody comes in?' Jean-Marc stammers.

'You can hide under the bed like a nice little mouse, you coward . . .'

It has to be said that the moment Jean-Marc sees me naked he changes his tune completely. He stops being scared of his own shadow. The way he looks then might even scare me if I didn't know how to make him meek as a lamb.

'Aren't you going to undress?' I say to him, falling on to the bed I've turned back.

76

He does so, tight-lipped. His prick is as hard and strong as those with which I endow the men in my dreams. He approaches the bed and even his awkwardness seems virile. He lies down beside me but is careful not to touch me. He knows me now. He knows he's not to take the initiative on his own. He looks at me, his hair ruffled, and with a glum expression. For the first time I have an urge for him to take me as Maurice did. I part my legs and raise my pubis gently. I draw my right hand across his cheek and pull his face nearer mine. I ask him to lie on top of me.

His body upon mine is amazingly light. I feel his prick and our stomachs press together – it's all very pleasant.

'You can do it inside me. But if you have the misfortune to come inside me, I'll never see you again. Do you understand? Never. I'll never speak to you again. You'll no longer exist, as far as I'm concerned. Understand?'

'I understand . . . Don't worry.'

He raises himself, takes his prick between his fingers and very deliberately plunges into my vagina, which is so moist that I scarcely feel him sink in. Yet I do, just, so softly and yet so hard that it's as if he himself is slithering inside me completely, like an eel in a stream . . . Slithering and shafting . . . A few years ago I overheard two boys in the street mentioning they were going to shaft a girl. Suddenly I understood what they meant. What they were saying disgusted me: I had the impression that not only was it bad but that it could injure you badly. I thought of fairground stalls where they give you a sort of wooden sword with which to unhook rings. And I imagined that shafting a girl meant sinking something hard like that wooden object into her stomach, no doubt to punish her for being a girl . . .

But today it's no punishment, certainly not! It's lovely. I look at Jean-Marc and he has tears in his eyes.

'I'm crazy about you, I love you Nea,' he murmurs.

I hold him tight and for a brief moment I admit I love him too. But of course I don't tell him so. And I think immediately of Maurice. It's Maurice I love, Maurice who loves me. Besides, I realize that Jean-Marc is on the point of climax. It's no time to lose my self-control. There. I shove both hands against his hips and force him off me. He heaves a sort of sigh of frustration. It's all right with me. He hasn't come yet anyway – I was too quick for him.

'Stay where you are,' I tell him.

He remains poised over me, resting on his tensed arms which are either side of me. His member is once again against my still wet, glistening pubis.

'Don't move.'

With my hand I make him come in a few seconds. Exactly what I wanted. His sperm makes a little lake of my navel.

'Now get off.'

'You want me to bring you a towel?' Jean-Marc asks.

'No, get dressed again. Go away.'

'You don't want me to stay.'

'You said it yourself, anyone might come in. Go on, I told you, don't get on my nerves, hurry up.'

Jean-Marc dresses again as quickly as he can. He makes as if to come and kiss me.

'No, please, get out . . .'

He's about to open the door. I call him back.

'Listen, Jean-Marc, if just *one* person even *suspects* what's happened between us, I'm warning you I'll hate you for ever, and that's final.'

'But why do you want . . .' Jean-Marc starts.

'I don't know, I'm simply warning you. Swear that you'll never say one word to any living person about what's happened.'

'Of course, Nea . . .'

'Promise.'

'I promise you, Nea.'

'On your own head be it?'

'On my head be it . . . And yours,' he adds with a sad little smile.

I too give him a smile and with a nod of my head show him the door. He goes.

I rise carefully, putting my hand to my belly to stop even one drop of Jean-Marc's sperm being lost. Very cautiously I make for my dressing-table. From it I pick up a tiny opal container in which I usually keep hairpins. I empty it and apply it to my stomach so the sperm runs into it. There's really quite a lot. That Jean-Marc!

I open the drawer and take out a very small segment of clingfilm I got from the kitchen this morning. Normally one uses the stuff for covering leftovers so they won't smell or lose flavour in the refrigerator. With it I cover the container. The sheet seals its edges hermetically. Perfect – I'm all set.

I read Walter Scott's *Quentin Durward* in its worn old wrapper for the third time. It's one of my favourites. I don't usually like Scott, he's too long-winded and I get fed up with the ethereal heroines. But they're nice love stories with happy endings. No matter what they say, stories that end badly are unpleasant. Yet when I'm reading the same thing always happens: I never realize how quickly the time is passing. I'm almost late. I hear water running in the bathroom. How can that be? Is Maurice having his shower already? Yes, that's it – as the parents are arriving he's somewhat earlier than usual in order to be ready on time. I must play for time.

I get up very quickly and go and knock on the bathroom door.

'Maurice, can you please let me in a moment, you're in plenty of time.'

Maurice grumbles but opens up. He's in his towelling robe and his hair is still wet. He moves aside to let me in and says:

'Hurry up, my clothes are on the chair and I'll have to come back in to get dressed.'

He goes into his room. I bolt the door. Yes, his clothes are there: thin black serge trousers, supple black suede snow-boots lined with lambswool, and a black cashmere rollneck sweater. He has carefully placed them upon a chair along with socks and briefs. I sit on the edge of the bath and look at my watch. It's ten to seven. There must be no mistakes. But I have calculated the timing carefully. Everything must go smoothly. I'll be hard put to it to find such ideal conditions again for going ahead with my plan.

At five to seven I open the door for Maurice, who gives me a black look but says nothing. What's going to happen when he finds his trousers covered in talcum powder! Even with a brush he'll have a hard job cleaning them as I've mixed water with the talc, so it won't be easy to remove. But I mustn't linger over details. If I want Maurice still to be in his dressing-gown I must hurry.

I stop in front of the wardrobe mirror and with both hands rip the front of my white silk blouse. I tear my brassière and then the tights. I have some trouble there, especially with the gusset, which is reinforced; also the material ladders everywhere but doesn't tear. Finally I manage it: not too bad.

Already I look quite dreadful. I mess up my hair and then things really do seem convincing. The most difficult part, though, is still to come. I part my legs. I stare at my reflection. I watch my hand moving down to my sex and try not to think, no longer to think about what I am doing. I watch as if this were a film: my hand sinks deep inside my sex and suddenly my nails are digging in, tearing ... The blood starts to flow.

Immediately I fling myself on to the bed, spreading my legs so that the blood soaks the sheets. I am so tense that I don't even feel the pain. The stinging I feel is as if buried deep inside my body. I turn my head towards the bedside table. The container with Jean-Marc's sperm is there and I take it, tear off the thin clingfilm covering it and turn it upside down into the palm of my hand. The sperm is cold, sticky. It rather disgusts me. I smear it across my thighs and the lips of my vagina. Several drops of it remain and these I wipe over the bed. Ready.

'Maurice, Maurice!'

I shout so loudly I get the same impression as five minutes earlier, when I saw myself in the mirror. It isn't I who cry out but somebody else. I don't recognize my voice, like when father recorded me on his tape recorder. I hear the first door, the bathroom one, opening, then the second, and Maurice is here. He halts on the threshold of my room and seems to hesitate.

'Maurice!'

I'm groaning and writhing on my bed. He's coming nearer.

'I feel so bad, Maurice, so bad.'

As I haven't switched on the lights there's just the light from the landing. He mustn't see me too clearly. He bends over me and start saying: 'Don't worry Nea, it's not serious, I'll go and get a ...'

What does he want to get? Whom? Mademoiselle Etchevery, Suzanne? To do what? To get rid of me once more and send me to hospital since he can't send me to boarding school. Get rid of me that way? I'll show him ...

'Nea, what's the matter with you?' he cries.

I don't reply. It's as if something is blocking my throat, I can no longer speak. I hate him, he frightens me. And suddenly I hear this awful shriek that shatters the whole house. Hear this cry I've just uttered at the top of my voice, as I tear and scratch at Maurice's face then push him off me, as far away from me as I can. I never want to see him again, never.

I close my eyes, hearing all sorts of noises, slamming doors, footsteps, running up the staircase that shakes the chalet's wooden walls. The door opens wide, the light is on and I open my eyes. They are all there: mother and father, the grocer's boy, Mademoiselle Etchevery, Monsieur Banat the taxi-driver, Suzanne, and of course, Maurice, his arms dangling by his sides and a wild look on his face all smeared with blood. I throw myself across the bed, my arms splayed out, looking at them all. How ashamed and frightened I am, and I feel the tears run down my face, the snot dribbling from my nose and into my mouth. How has all this happened? What's happened?

'Why did you do it, Maurice? Why, why? Tell me ... Maurice, it hurts. Oh mummy!'

Chapter V

THE KNIFE FOR OPENING EYES

*I was desperate. Was I really dead? I had to know, at all costs,
even at the price of the greatest suffering.*
I took and unfastened the knife for opening eyes.

Henri Michaux: *Morte-Moronne*

I've never seen father so pale.

Mother throws herself on me and pulls me off the bed.
She hurts me, twisting my wrist. I don't know what possesses
her. She drags me into the bathroom and thrusts me almost
brutally into a towelling bathrobe. I can't swear to it, but her
expression is of disgust more than anything. I've already
mentioned that mother doesn't like what she calls 'that sort
of thing'. I really believe she has it in for me quite as much
as for Maurice. But she pulls herself together, clasps me
against her and when I look up I'm surprised to see tears
trickling down her face. Her arms are around me. She hugs
me close, giving me little pats on the back and murmuring
into my hair: 'My poor darling, my poor girl ... what a
horrible thing!'

At that, suddenly it's my turn to cry. Until I can't weep
any more. What have I done? I realize I've crossed a
threshold. I'll never be able to go back, I'll never be the
same. I can't ever tell them it's not true, that Maurice has
done nothing, that I've imagined it all ... I can't ever ... I'm
scared, scared someone will expose my lie. That would be
terrible, what would happen to me? It's not all my fault
anyway. Why did Maurice hurt me so? I loved him. I only
wanted to live in his shadow. It wasn't so difficult, all it

would have taken was for him to ask my parents if I could go and live at their place. I'd have been happy with that. I'm sure Suzanne would have been happy. But that's what we should have done. I ought to have said I wanted to go and live with Suzanne. Perhaps it's still possible? Maybe if I ask now, everyone could turn a blind eye to this whole business? I'll explain to them that Maurice didn't mean me any harm, that he entered my room by mistake, tripped and fell on the bed, and I was scared and screamed like an idiot. I'll tell them something anyhow. I'll show them Maurice meant no harm . . .

'You know mother, Maurice didn't mean to hurt me . . .'

'Shut up, Nea! . . . Oh, I'm sorry darling . . . Don't talk dear, don't say a thing. You've been hurt. You must forget what's happened, that's all there is to it . . .'

'But mother, I swear to you . . .!'

'Come on, Nea. Maurice has committed a dreadful crime. He's a monster. You mustn't even utter his name . . . just forget his existence . . .'

Poor mother. It's not that simple. For a start they try to get him right out of the way. I don't see the Fribourg police when they come for Maurice. I see hardly anyone that day. Mother takes me into her room and insists I lie down there. Dr Soulier comes. I know him, he was called last year when I had laryngitis and my throat hurt. He calls me Mademoiselle Nea and while examining me teases me slyly because I think once someone told him I was a good student: 'You mustn't become a bluestocking. A pretty girl like you should learn to sew and cook, that's more important than Latin and Maths. Doctor's orders, Mademoiselle Nea.'

Today he's not joking. He takes my pulse.

'I must give you a little gynaecological examination, Mademoiselle Nea. It won't hurt.'

I dread that, yet I'm not worried – quite the opposite. He takes a small glass slide and on it smears the samples with a wooden spatula. I've allowed for that.

84

When he's finished, he gives me an injection and two tablets to take with a glass of water. I fall asleep dreaming of an owl. I don't realize that for years I'll always associate Maurice's face with that of an owl: I think it's to do with the shape of the eyes.

As for forgetting! Mother didn't reckon with the inquiry. I heard my parents and the police first, then the examining magistrate later, carrying on endlessly down in the main room of the chalet. Finally mother must have given in and the examining magistrate came to ask me questions in my room. And what a swine he was!

Mother wanted to be present during the interrogation. He refused, so there was just him and his clerk in the room with me. They sat near my bed, then the magistrate in his flat, excessively polite voice began. Monsieur Mignot his clerk kept rubbing his hands throughout the questioning, as if seeking to recharge some kind of energy, like an athlete doing exercises between events.

I don't know why, but I looked at that clerk first. I was scared of the magistrate, yet I felt that Mignot, because I'd heard his name correctly from the start, was – unlike him – just an average sort of man. The sort of person who would trust me.

He had a sympathetic expression, what was more, and that reassured me as he wrote away conscientiously on his clipboard.

The magistrate's name, Amédée Violle, I only caught a few days later, when father mentioned that on mother's request he had approached the President of the Cantonal Tribunal in order to persuade him to curb this man's immoderate zeal.

Mother thought those repetitious interrogations from which I would often return in tears were bad enough for me. But of course the President of the Cantonal Tribunal gave father a courteous brush-off, reminding him that an examining magistrate was answerable to nobody and that Judge Violle was far more conscientious regarding his juridical prerogatives than almost any other of his colleagues. Father bowed to this, but mother continued to feel it unbecoming that a man of father's importance couldn't get them to leave me in peace: wasn't I after all the victim?

I suspect that it was precisely on this point that Judge Violle had his doubts. Even today I still think he guessed everything right from my very first cross-examination. I'll never know why, but from his opening question on I was convinced he didn't believe a word I said.

Immediately after the identification questioning, the magistrate asked me to recount to him in detail all that had happened. I kept to the facts that could be verified by everyone my screams had summoned – father, mother, and the various friends accompanying them. Maurice had entered my room, come over to my bed, bent over me; no doubt he'd intended to kiss me and then, suddenly, he'd done some strange things that had taken me by surprise; he'd grabbed my wrists and lain on top of me and really hurt me, hurt me a lot. I'd cried out, struggled, remembered nothing more...

The detail about Maurice grabbing my wrists was the first point Judge Violle dwelt upon.

'How were you able to scratch Maurice Puiseux's face and chest if he were gripping your wrists?'

'Well, first of all he was holding my wrists and then he must have let go of them – how can I remember?'

'If he let go of you, was that because you were no longer struggling?'

'No, quite the opposite, I was trying to get up, to get off the bed ... and yes, I remember now ... he let go of my wrists and placed both hands on my shoulders, I remember it clearly, put both hands on my shoulders to push me down again.'

'But if he forced you to lie down again, weren't you frightened, or angry with him? Now you told me a short while back that you didn't think he wanted to do wrong, that you were sure he had considerable affection for you . . .'

'That's right, Maurice has always been very nice to me. Afraid? No, I was furious . . . Well, I suppose I *was* afraid . . . What I meant was, I didn't blame him, I didn't think he wanted to do anything bad . . . But it really hurt though. I screamed because I'd been hurt . . . I didn't want to scratch him and I didn't know I was scratching him . . . I didn't want to hurt him, I was just struggling . . . it was like in an argument, when my sister Suzanne was younger and sometimes we'd fight. Mother used to say we fought like washerwomen. I remember I once scratched Suzanne, but I didn't realize I'd done it . . . It was like that with Maurice.'

'And do you often quarrel with your sister Suzanne?'

'Not often. Not at all – I love my sister a lot. We're both very close. She says I'm her friend, in spite of the age difference . . .'

'But aren't you upset that she got married? You didn't want her to, did you?'

'Oh no your honour, I was so happy! On the contrary, you don't know how lovely the wedding was – and Maurice was so nice too.'

'Aren't you rather unhappy though, that she has left you? Don't you bear a grudge against your brother-in-law for coming between you?'

'No, not at all, your honour, Maurice likes me a lot. You see by marrying Suzanne he can see even more of me.'

'And are *you* happy to see more of him?'

'That's not quite what I meant, sir. But we're all very close. What I meant was, he is one of the family. We are very happy, I'm very happy. It's true.'

Judge Violle cross-questioned Suzanne for a long time after that. I must say Suzanne surprised me there. In her shoes I don't know if I'd have reacted at all like she did, but she told us herself that she never wanted to hear Maurice's name again, it was as simple as that. She'd developed an aversion towards him, so she reacted as if he'd always been a complete stranger to her. She explained to our parents that she confined herself to answering all the magistrate's questions by saying that she and Maurice had never had any physical relations, that she'd never truly been his wife. Mother tried to send me out of the room when she touched upon this aspect of their relationship, yet after telling me once to go to my room no one, in the heat of the conversation, took any further notice of me. They went on talking and didn't bother to mince words:

'You didn't tell him you'd never slept with your husband did you?' Mother exclaimed.

'Of course I did!' Suzanne said. 'Anyhow, it's as if I never had. That swine, that filthy swine! I feel sick to think of him even touching me!'

'I don't know if you realize, Suzanne dear,' said mother, 'but certain things one knows one can't conceal. When a man and a woman ...'

'Mother, please! Don't give me a sex education lecture! But you didn't really imagine I was a virgin when I married Maurice, did you? I slept with a whole string of men, but never with Maurice! Anyway, that's what I told the judge, because he had the same reaction as you when I told him Maurice hadn't done it once to me. Then I said to him "Well, you can get your nurses to examine me whenever you please, but I'm telling you again that nothing happened between Maurice and myself." '

'My dear Suzanne, I don't see where these extraordinary statements of yours are going to get you.'

'To a divorce, father ... annulment. Maurice has never existed as far as I'm concerned. Never. I don't ever want to hear him discussed again and that's final!'

Quite obviously this bizarre confession of Suzanne's constituted one more charge against Maurice. Clearly anything might be expected of a man whose wife refuses consummation. Years later I found out that this was one point, , like so many others, which Maurice disputed hotly, and that he swore Suzanne was lying. He described their sexual relations in such extravagant detail that even his sincerity was held against him. His 'imaginative excesses' could well have been the products of frustration: caught between my statements and Suzanne's violent revulsion, Maurice found himself completely trapped, nailed like an owl to a barn door and exposed for everyone to see.

But Judge Violle didn't admit defeat. He always kept coming back to me in the long run. I must have stayed in that chalet with my parents well past the end of the holidays. He insisted on enforcing all the necessary procedures of the inquiry, and my parents organized a sort of correspondence course for me with my various teachers. It seemed I was an interesting victim and everybody wanted to help me out – especially Maître Jarrot my lawyer. Indeed it was my parents who arranged for a lawyer to be present during the cross-examinations. They foresaw and stressed a score of psychological consequences resulting from the rape. Without realizing the deep-seated reasons for it, they sensed the examining magistrate's hostility and were indignant about it.

As was Maître Jarrot. I realized at once that I had to have a genuine ally. When he too put questions to me, very politely and kindly, so as to reconstruct what had happened, I gave him a very different account from the one I'd told the examining magistrate. I liked this lawyer a lot: he was tall, with chestnut hair, and I thought him very distinguished with his fine hazel eyes and their long black lashes. Perhaps he was just a little overweight, but far from being unbecoming, this slight obesity lent him a certain shyness. Mother, who always knows everybody's background, said that he came from a good Fribourg family. Knowing as he did the class

89

origins of most people in the Canton, he took a dislike to Judge Violle from the start: the two men clearly did not move in the same social circles, said mother in the prissy voice she adopted for coffee mornings. Maître Jarrot was a well known figure abroad, father maintained, going one better. He went to France several times a month, spoke English, too. Mother and father had met him on various occasions in the company of mutual friends. That was why they had the idea of getting him to represent us.

As for Judge Violle, he was a petty bureaucrat. His mother was a German Swiss and he spoke a heavily accented French. He clearly distrusted men like father and Maître Jarrot, and ever since the lawyer began attending my cross-examinations there were invariably some sharp exchanges between them. Maître Jarrot would wax indignant over the examining magistrate's brusque manner and he himself would each time drily point out that in the investigation of a crime only the truth deserved respect.

As far as I'm concerned the strange thing is that though I've charmed Maître Jarrot and know it, I've also taken a liking to Judge Violle at the same time as I'm afraid of him. He's my match, whereas with Maître Jarrot it's all too easy. Now when the latter comes to fetch me for an interview, I kiss him on both cheeks like my parents. Then he takes my hand and I stare at him wide-eyed with my innocent expression, the expression I adopt without difficulty because all it takes is for me to think about my innocence and feel that my questioners believe in it too. I can switch it on and off at will, and that makes me feel so good that it's as if I'm bathed in a rosy glow. Which is what they like too and what makes me appealing.

But nothing works on Judge Violle. I try in vain to disconcert him with my stare, my lips parted as if breathless. No good either answering him as sweetly as I can, looking straight at him – nothing reaches him. Judge Violle is short. His head comes up to Maître Jarrot's shoulder. His hair, too close-cropped, has a parting on one side. His ears stick out too much and his bony fretful features resemble certain portraits I've seen at the Louvre painted by Renaissance artists: bankers, for instance, pictured beside scales and gold pieces, or merchants in fluted ruffs. He never smiles, yet something tells me that if one could get past his chilly exterior he might be very nice, sweet, far sweeter than Maître Jarrot. Maître Jarrot in naïve rather than sweet. He can't have had many difficulties as a child nor as a young man, nor throughout his career. It's odd but he reminds me of Jean-Marc.

Jean-Marc is only a kid; Maître Jarrot is very masculine, he even has a certain charm, a presence, whereas Jean-Marc is introverted and not really at ease. The first time Jean-Marc saw me again after the 'rape' he stared at me strangely; he must have remembered about the sperm, but it never occurred to him that I might have set things up so Maurice would fall into the trap. A vague doubt must have surfaced somewhere, but not one he could define. He's tried to talk to me about it, but throughout this whole affair I've seen to it that we've never been alone together. When the holiday ended, he went back. He did manage to find the opportunity when we saw him off on the Lausanne train to stammer into my ear: 'I really don't understand! I'm sorry, it's awful! Do you think . . .' I didn't let him finish. As far as I'm concerned, *he's* finished. Jean-Marc represents 'before'. Now I have too many other things to think about.

I must work: no, work isn't the word . . . I must prepare myself. That's what I feel, yet how to explain it: I must prepare myself for Maurice.

At present I'm still not very sure of what I'm looking for or what I want, but Maurice is there in all my thoughts, my actions, my fantasies. I only see him, like a beacon, shining and dazzling.

So the night after his arrest, before going to sleep I caress myself as if nothing has ever happened: I'm stretched out stiffly upon my bed and my feet are cold. I feel I want to cry or even die (it's not really a death wish, but the feeling that death might not be too far off), and at the same time my hand cannot leave my vagina, my triangle. My finger slides between the outer lips. I'd like to be in the street, caressing myself in full view of everyone and the moment I think this, 'everyone' becomes Maurice.

In the darkness I close my eyes in order to make it still darker, and imagine the street teeming with men and women. They stop to look at me caressing myself: standing in the corner of a doorway I am facing them, and then after a moment a man draws nearer and this man is Maurice. He approaches me and I see only him, he sees only me, and when he's facing me he slowly undoes the belt of his trousers, unzips his fly to expose his erect penis to me. He takes it in his hand and draws still closer and I come before even thinking that he's going to penetrate me. Maybe I don't really want him to penetrate me; I think what I like is his hand gripping his swollen and erect penis which points at my own sex; what I like best are his eyes that are drawn towards my vagina, his pupils that seem to emit an incandescence and are like laser beams focusing upon the tip of my clitoris, that tiny bud on which I'm pressing so urgently . . .

Every time Maître Jarrot comes to visit me, I think of Jean-Marc and Maurice simultaneously. Every day he comes to collect me and take me along to the examining magistrate. Mother shows him up to my room. He sits on a small stool beside my wardrobe with the mirror on it. I stay lying on the bed, I turn over the book I've been reading and I listen to him. When talking to me he uses a special tone, very kind and soft, and he explains the law to me and what the judge expects of me. He prepares me and questions me too, not so much about what has happened, since he is, or thinks he is, perfectly well informed on that score, but more about myself and my feelings. I'm sure my parents have persuaded him to set me on the straight and narrow once again. I know how they think, they must imagine that I'm deeply disturbed, and I realize only too well that my manner must seem to be quite different from before.

I've worked out a really amazing trick, something that goes much better than I could have expected. I tell him that since Maurice's attack I've felt a sort of burning between my thighs. He flushes when I mentioned it to him and says to me very hastily:

'Have you talked to the doctor about it, Nea?'

'No, that's not what I meant, Maître, it's a burning sensation, a sort of memory I experience. I have to admit that it's almost pleasant, but I'm very ashamed about it.'

'You mustn't be ashamed. The only person who should die of shame, and I do literally mean die, is Maurice.'

'Oh no, Maurice mustn't die! I already told you, Maître, I'm sure he didn't mean me harm. You see I know he loved me and I loved Maurice very much too. Besides, if it weren't true, I wouldn't have this . . . pleasant . . . memory.'

I pause before saying 'pleasant' and watch him. I feel it upsets him. Already the burning feeling I mentioned has had a strange effect on him, but I realize that by talking of a pleasant sensation I am embarrassing him terribly and I, on the contrary, find this idea enjoyable. While uttering the word 'pleasant' I really did feel that warmth again, the same warmth and moistness within my vagina which, when I'm alone, makes me caress myself straight away, no matter when or how.

Maître Jarrot advises me not to speak of this sensation to the magistrate.

'I'm not suggesting you should hide anything, Nea, but believe me, a judge doesn't have to know your inmost thoughts and feelings and sensations – they belong to you and only you.'

'But I can talk about them to you, can't I?' I ask him innocently.

'Of course,' he says with some difficulty, opening his mouth as if to add something, then lapsing into silence, placing both hands on my shoulders and looking into my eyes. Then he leaves.

The kinder Maître Jarrot is to me, the nastier the examining magistrate becomes. When Maître Jarrot once again protests about the innumerable inquisitions I'm made to endure, the judge answers him drily:

'Don't worry, Maître, this examination is the last. It can only end in Maurice Puiseux's committal proceedings ... or else I'd be obliged to find no grounds for prosecution.'

'What's that?' Maître Jarrot chokes. 'No grounds? ... After all the dreadful ordeals my client has undergone, the nervous and psychological upheavals whose consequences may scar her for the rest of her life!'

'Don't get carried away, Maître,' the examining magistrate interrupts calmly. 'I confined myself to showing you that the evidence assembled must logically lead to Maurice Puiseux's committal unless, of course, some new factor – I grant you rather unlikely at this stage of our inquiry – is produced to establish his innocence.'

While uttering these words, the judge stares pointedly at me.

'That's the limit!' Maître Jarrot bursts out. 'New factor, what new factor, your honour? He was caught in the act!'

'Not exactly *in flagrante delicto*, Maître ... All the testimonies in my possession, other than Mademoiselle's, could be termed *a posteriori*. Thus the alleged crime ...'

'Scarcely alleged, but established by irrefutable material proof!' Maître Jarrot cuts in.

'By that you mean circumstantial evidence of a substantial nature,' the magistrate corrects him, still very calmly, and continuing to look at me.

'All the same, your honour,' Maître Jarrot goes on heatedly, 'how would you categorize the marks inflicted by my client on her attacker's face and,' he adds lowering his eyes and voice, 'the evidence of the unspeakable indignities she was forced to endure?'

In the meanwhile, however, I have not lowered my gaze. I go on staring the magistrate in the face. I know he doesn't believe me and never has done. He's trying to intimidate me. He doesn't know me. Everyone in authority, every teacher I've ever had, has tried the same trick when they can't prove something, they affirm it. But I've always stuck to my story and haven't been caught out.

The magistrate sighs and resumes:

'Mademoiselle, I have here before me a summary of your statements, and I'm going to ask you for one last time to tell us in detail what happened on the evening of the 30th December from seven fifteen onwards.'

Maître Jarrot protests yet again, but I cut short his fine phrases and state in my sweetest tones that I am ready to do whatever the magistrate requires. I talk for almost ten minutes. He checks out the minutest details over and over again. My memory is crystal clear. As I'm finishing I see that the magistrate would like to ask me still more questions. He opens his mouth and then I know he's changed his mind because for the first time since I've been sitting there he has stopped looking me in the eyes. He turns towards Maître Jarrot.

'As I told you, Maître, you had no need to worry: this final examination could only result in the referral of this affair to the Court at Bulle. I have the honour of informing you accordingly that tomorrow I shall hand over the file to the Public Prosecutor ... I assume you have nothing further to add, Mademoiselle.'

He turns towards me again, without looking at me.

I place my hand on Maître Jarrot's arm and look at him half-apologetically before again meeting the magistrate's gaze:

'I don't know if I should say this to you, but I really think I must . . . Maurice didn't want to harm me, I've always told you that, and if he didn't want to hurt me, one can't talk of rape, can one?'

I'm sitting up very straight and I know (it's something I learned very early) that in this position, when I straighten my back my breasts, though small, are clearly defined under my pullover. And since mother likes me to wear rather short pleated skirts, whenever I sit in this way my knees are exposed. Mother always says my knees are very attractive, not, she adds, those frightful scrawny knees that are a woman's bane.

'So your honour, how can I explain? I tried to tell Maître Jarrot, but he didn't want me to bore you with my feelings and ideas. He told me you wouldn't want to hear all that from me. But it's true that from that moment, right until today . . . every day since . . . since Maurice . . .'

'Since the thirtieth of December, Mademoiselle!' the magistrate interrupts icily.

'Yes sir, since the thirtieth. I wasn't hurt, and not only that . . . as I tell you this, I put my right hand against my . . . stomach . . . and I have to admit, it's true I'm rather ashamed, but I feel a sort of nice warmth . . .'

'Your honour, you yourself said this file is now closed. My client's comments only make it abundantly clear how frightful was the psychological damage caused by Maurice Puiseux. I ask you to allow us to retire at once.'

The examining magistrate has a funny lopsided smile on his face. He bows his head and rests his forehead for a moment in his hands. Then he stares at me again lengthily without saying anything. Finally, rising slowly to his feet, he says:

'You're absolutely right, Maître. As things stand there is no more to be said and nothing your client may add can change the evidence that has prompted the indictment of Maurice Puiseux. You may withdraw.'

As soon as we find ourselves back in the street, Maître

Jarrot takes me to task. I look appropriately chastened. Yet I know all too well that the magistrate was angry with me but could do nothing. Deep down that man despises me and regards me as a dirty little liar. In the long run, though, he's been the one to lose his cool. Just the same, I'm a bit fed up with Maître Jarrot: I don't like the sharp way he treated me. Anyway, for all his paternal manner, I'm sure he's just like the rest. We arrive back and he follows me into the main room of the chalet. I'll soon find out about that last point.

'Look,' I tell him, holding out a folded note I've just found beside the telephone, 'it's my mother, she says here she's served tea in my room and she'll be back shortly. If you'd like to come up and have a cup of tea with me, we can wait for her together.'

He declines, but I let him know that mother will certainly be disappointed not to see him, and finally he agrees. We go upstairs and I offer him a small easy-chair near my dressing table – upon which mother has left a tea-tray.

'See, I was right ...'

I show him the three cups beside the teapot.

'The third cup is obviously for you. Mother'll be cross if you don't stay.'

I help him off with his coat, fill his cup and give him a cake. Poor Maître Jarrot really looks pleased. He contemplates me with an expression almost as silly as Jean-Marc's.

'You've been very brave, my dear Nea,' he says softly. 'Now you must forget it all. There'll be one more difficult time, with the trial, but you'll see, it won't last long, and then it really will be over and done with.'

'Don't worry, Maître, everything'll be all right ... I'm just going to the bathroom for a minute and I'll be back. Make yourself at home. I'm sure mother won't be long.'

I'm positive this Maître Jarrot with his sugar daddy manner is just like all the rest. I'll clear this little matter up right away.

I open the door leading to the bathroom and glance

behind me. As I thought, sitting where he now is, Maître Jarrot can see via my wardrobe mirror everything going on in the bathroom between bath and basin. The very place where there's a small low wicker chair on which I sit to take off my stockings. Seated where I am I can no longer see him, but I know that the lower half of my body is reflected in the mirror in front of him. So I take off my tiny briefs and hike up my skirt. I stroke my buttocks a bit in passing and spread my legs. I often caress myself in this position, but of course on other occasions I bolt the door.

To begin with I think about the examining magistrate and what I told him. I'm sure that when I spoke of the warmth and that pleasant burning I keep feeling, it must have had some effect upon him. It must have had an effect on him akin to that which Maître Jarrot is experiencing now, as he sits over there, saying nothing of course, and of course, not moving. After all, if what he's seeing upsets or shocks him he need only leave his chair. He only has to get up and shut the door of my room. But no, he's careful to stay put and I'm sure he sees, is watching. It disgusts me and yet pleases me to think so. It disgusts me because it reminds me of Maurice, I don't know why, and of Jean-Marc, and of all these men who read a dirty meaning into everything. But my getting indignant about it is quite enjoyable also, and since everyone is like that, why aren't I too? Is he looking at me? Well, I'm glad he is. Glad his eyes can't tear themselves away from the mirror ... So with this in view when I put my hand to my vagina, I'm already so wet that it won't take long. I can't even hold back a slight moan when I come. Maybe he's heard it? The moment it's over though, I've had enough, I'm no longer interested. Only one thing interests me, knowing how my upright lawyer is, out there. I put my slip back on again at top speed, quickly run a comb through my hair, dab a little scent on my face and return to the room, completely natural.

'Hasn't my mother arrived?'

'No, Nea,' he answers in a very low and rather shaky voice. 'No. But I think I should be going ...'

He makes as if to get up.

'Of course you mustn't, Maître!' I laugh. 'I know a good way to stop you ...'

This way is simply by jumping into his lap and thus finding out pronto whether Maître Jarrot is as decent and respectable as one supposes. While I kiss him on both cheeks girlishly, clasping my hands behind his back, I can feel under my haunches that he too, like Maurice and Jean-Marc, has a huge hard member, a member which could sink into my vagina in search of its own pleasure.

I was right: he's like all the rest of them. Everybody's alike. So why, pray, is Maurice being threatened with jail for doing what anyone would have done in his place? Why do some go to prison and others remain free? Why does everybody seem to pity me so much when they all want the very same thing? Even my parents ... After all, if they hadn't done the selfsame thing, I wouldn't be here ...

It's I who pity them all. I who now know I can make any of them do those things they all claim to find so dirty and unpleasant.

PART TWO

THE BURNING SNOW

This land is so luminous that it resembles snowflakes on fire.
Cyrano de Bergerac: *Other Worlds*

Chapter VI

THE REVERSE OF A LIE

Well, OK for prison, it was all that was lacking to make a hero out of me.

Jean Paulhan: *Famous Trials*

I'm huddled into my corner. I have the impression that my head is balanced on the collar of my cape, detached from the rest of my body, like one of those small bunches of tissue paper from which are made petticoat dolls, angels and gnomes for Christmas trees. My cape buttons are fastened. It forms a brown cone all around me.

From the position in which I'm sitting my feet are not visible. My hands, folded upon my stomach, cannot be seen. I am completely motionless. I like this cape very much. Mother bought it for me from the Marie-Martine boutique in the Rue de Sèvres. It gives me an old-fashioned look. It's smooth as silk if stroked the right way, and when one does so against the nap it stands out like animal fur.

Mademoiselle Pommard or Pommaud is seated next to me. It isn't a difficult name but I've never been able to get it quite right. Today I'm wondering whether it isn't actually just Pommier. She has a fat colourless face surrounded by streaky blonde curls upon which is perched a man's bottle green leather hat with a feather, green too, like her suit, her woollen stockings and her court shoes with big brass buckles. I remember, because she talks about them on the slightest pretext, that those stockings are specially for sufferers from varicose veins.

She is assistant to Professor Jungsfeld, the director of a centre of 'recuperative psychotherapy' at Romont near Fribourg. Frankly this must be a nuthouse, or as mother would say, a place for highly-strung people. Like most people, I've since read Jungsfeld's famous book, *Second Wind: fifteen cases of psycho-resuscitation.*

I'm in charge. Father, who knows everybody, got the professor to let her stay with us throughout Maurice's trial. It's no use their talking behind my back, I understand everything they say. They're worried about the psychological effect the court case may have on me. I'm not.

It must be two hours since the first hearing began in the Courthouse at Bulle. I haven't even caught a glimpse of the courtroom. All the witnesses have been led into an adjoining room and we aren't allowed to be present during the proceedings until summoned to testify. The whole of Charmey seems to have turned out: Monsieur Banat the taxi driver who drove mother and father from Lausanne that fateful evening; Mademoiselle Etchevery and two or three more tradespeople whose names I don't know.

Suzanne sits quite alone in a corner of the room. She hardly speaks to me ... She hardly speaks to anyone any more.

Mother and father, next to each other, a foot or two away from me, aren't looking at me. Father's head is in his hands, his elbows resting on his knees. Mother, by contrast, beautifully dressed and made up, sits very stiffly staring at the wall. From time to time I see her lips move. It's one of her tics when she wants to remember something, not to omit anything from her shopping list.

Four or five policemen are standing in a group in another corner, busily discussing the trial in murmurs. I can't hear anything they say. It's very hot. I know this is going to take a long time. Maître Jarrot has warned me that I'll almost certainly be the last witness.

The police officers are called first. An usher opens the

door and they disappear one by one. All the Charmey people queue up in single file. It is father's turn, then mother's. She gives me a little wave before leaving the room, wearing her nice pre-exams smile. Suzanne passes right by me as if unseeing, then it's my turn at last.

When I enter the courtroom I see the two swing doors of the main entrance that face the rostrum on which the circuit judge is seated, flanked by four assessors, and the counsels' benches and the dock, noiselessly swinging back shut. The room has just been cleared.

I've been expecting that. Maître Jarrot warned me that as I'm only sixteen the judge will hear my testimony *in camera*. Only the witnesses and Maître Jarrot remain in the courtroom. He is representing father, who has instituted the civil action.

By special permission of the court, Mademoiselle Pommaud or Pommier, has been authorized to accompany me. She doesn't come into the witness box with me but sits below it and gives me what she imagines is an encouraging smile, a sort of sugary lollipop vendor's grimace.

'Don't be disturbed, Mademoiselle, everyone here present ... I say everyone advisedly,' the judge opens, glancing significantly towards the dock where Maurice is sitting, 'everyone present well understands how painful it is for you to be here. First of all I must ask you to tell us clearly your Christian and surnames.'

I'm used to it. It's no more nerve-wracking than an exam. Quite the contrary. In an exam the teachers wait to get their revenge on you. Here whoever is the cleverest wins. They aren't like that awful examining magistrate. They don't treat me like a liar. I'm really glad.

I'm sworn in and tell the story of the rape, which I now know by heart. I'm not anxious or worried, but I haven't foreseen the look on Maurice's face.

To begin with I look at him as if he doesn't exist. Or rather, which isn't so difficult, as if he is just a presence or a waxwork dummy. I can even turn towards the dock two or three times in succession. I look at his hands in particular. I notice he's dressed to the nines: so smart in his navy-blue suit, his white shirt and dark blue tie with tiny white polka dots – his 'Old Boys' and young officer's outfit' as I'd joke to him. He's had a good haircut and has been so well shaved that I can almost smell his aftershave. Something else I used to joke about: he uses *Scar*, and each time I recognized the scent I'd call him my darling pirate.

I mention these details although they form a series of images of Maurice superimposed one on the other: it isn't really Maurice himself.

And then I catch his eye. I've always liked Maurice's eyes, those big round eyes with their network of tiny wrinkles that give him a very wise yet at the same time mocking expression. The look of a fairy-tale uncle, not really the eyes of a human being. They are round rather than oval and he has long, thick but delicate lashes, like the sable paintbrushes one uses for watercolours.

Catching his eye, I am taken by surprise. I know him so well. I thought he'd have a tragic yet reproachful expression. He can look so very dignified when he wants to. But instead I am sucked down into a whirlpool. I am standing at least seven or eight yards away from him, maybe further, but I can see only his pupils, not even the eyes, his pupils . . . I see his eyes as if from the outside and then I enter through his pupils, sucked into a whirlpool. In the depth of his pupils black as Indian ink something tears at my heartstrings.

He's there, still there. He hasn't moved at all, still the same distance away, very far, very close. Standing engulfed by my conical cape I feel I've already been guillotined. How silly I am, Switzerland doesn't have the guillotine! But my head's been cut off, my heart pierced, I'm transfixed by a needle that has pierced me during this descent into the abyss.

Why is he looking at me like that?

I answer the judge, I speak, am incapable of remembering a single word of what I say. My head is talking, only my head, perched above my cape, and underneath I am burning.

Suddenly the prosecutor rises and points at Maurice, shouting:

'So, do you still deny everything? Can you listen without shuddering to the evidence of this young woman you have sullied?'

Maurice leaps to his feet. He's not looking at me any longer, he's once more that smooth conventional Maurice I've always known, only gripped by a new vehemence ... I no longer see his eyes, he's only a gesticulating shadow. Standing facing the judge, the jury and the public prosecutor, he yells:

'I swear I'm innocent, I've always said so and I'm telling you again. Innocent ... This is a ridiculous fabrication, a group of circumstances, a ... I don't know what it is. Nea, I don't know what you've said or done, I really don't understand ... I beg you ... I had a good life, a wife, Suzanne. What has she said? Why has she turned against me too? Why doesn't she believe me? And all of you, you know me ... it's crazy, all this, mad ...'

'Calm yourself,' the prosecutor interrupts briskly. 'This disorderly outburst will not assist your case.'

'But I'm not going to let you have your way,' Maurice rages, 'not going to let you destroy me ...'

'And did *you* hesitate to destroy the integrity of another human being?'

They can't go on like this, it's so stupid. Right, Maurice did exaggerate, he shouldn't have dropped me like he did, but they're absurd with their highfaluting waffle.

'I'd like to say something ...'

'Witness has told us everything necessary,' protests the prosecutor, giving me that look I know so well, the one used by teachers or the headmistress of the *lycée* when they address you in front of your parents, that benevolent look

107

... You bet I know it ... And I know them too: the moment they're alone together, they'll bitch away.

'If this young lady thinks she can provide us with any further relevant details, the court must hear her out,' the judge rules.

He himself seems quite nice. He glances at me kindly. He believes me. I'm sure that if I were alone I could explain in detail to him how everything happened and he would understand ... But that is no longer possible. All the same, I'm not going to let myself be treated like a liar all my life by characters like this prosecutor just because once and once only I haven't told the truth ... I can try to get Maurice out of this masquerade, otherwise ... One needn't have magical powers to do that much, surely. They're so stupid ...

'What I wanted to say, your honour ...'

'Face the ladies and gentlemen of the jury,' the judge directs me quietly. 'It is to them you are speaking.'

'Maurice is right. Everything said about him is untrue. Even Suzanne hasn't described things the way they are. Maurice has always been very nice. Mother doesn't like him at all, she dislikes commercial representatives. But father has always defended him, father knows him. And I don't want to attack Suzanne, she *is* my sister, but she was lucky to get Maurice. I ...'

I'm on the wrong track. I'm about to say that if Maurice has given me so much happiness, so much love, Suzanne should have been even happier than I ... But that wouldn't be a good idea. They wouldn't understand at all. I wouldn't be allowed to finish and Mademoiselle Pommier would explain once more that I have suffered a severe trauma.

'Maurice wouldn't hurt a fly. I swear to you he liked me a lot. He helped me more than once with my homework. Thanks to him, really, I came top in Maths ... That's not the point today, I realize ... but nobody forced him to do that. It so happens that I do argue and even fight with people I like a lot ... Suzanne, for instance. We've fought each other often. She gave me a black eye two years ago, and she meant it, while I scratched the whole of her left shoulder till it bled. Nobody sent us to prison. You can't call either of us monsters. It's possible I got Maurice into a temper without my realizing it. Mother is the first to say I'm strong-willed. And it's true that Maurice had been annoying me for several days, so I decided to pay him back.'

'Why?' asks the judge.

'I don't know ... We were on holiday and there weren't many people around at the chalet. I wanted us all to have a good laugh together as we usually did. He didn't even notice me. That annoyed me. Frankly I was horrible to him, and not just to him. Ask the others, I was awful to Jean-Marc too ... Maurice had had enough of it, that's all, he jumped on top of me, I was half asleep, I was scared, it was my fault I was stupid ...'

'Your honour,' the prosecutor exclaims, rising abruptly to his feet, 'the candour of this young woman, her ignorance of the borderland where lust replaces violence, condemn the hateful creature her kind heart prompts her to defend. This plea damns you, sir, even more emphatically than her accusations. Don't you feel it?'

He points a finger at Maurice, who is very pale This prosecutor has begun to irritate me. I know what I'm saying, I'm not a cretin.

'He is good, your honour,' I say, looking Maurice in the face so that he will know this time I am not lying.

I love Maurice. More than Suzanne, anyhow. She doesn't give a damn about him. The moment he was accused – and he is after all her husband – she's had only one thought, escape. I'm sure she's already thinking of finding someone else. That's just like her. She doesn't love me any more either. She loves no one. And *I* love Maurice. He didn't realize it immediately. Instead of making him understand, I wanted my revenge ...

'I've been wicked ... Please forgive me, Maurice, I'm sure

you didn't want to hurt me. I know you didn't want to hurt me ... I ...'

'Shut up, Nea.'

Maurice suddenly sits bolt upright. He's looking at me but no longer with his kindly owlish look or his salesman-visiting-important-client expression: no, he's looking at *me*. He stares at me as he did the day I became his wife, stares at me as if I were touching him. He continues in a very odd, shaky, rasping voice.

'You're right, gentlemen ... You shouldn't let her say any more ... Believe me, I'm absolutely innocent of everything I'm accused of. But Nea shouldn't ever have come into this courtroom or heard all these horrible things. I beg you, your honour ...'

'Very well,' the judge retorts almost hesitantly, 'go back to your seat, Mademoiselle.'

At lunch the next day my father says he thinks the afternoon session will be the last. There'll be the prosecution summing up and the speech by Maurice's counsel, a self-satisfied Parisian with an enormous Legion of Honour decoration on his black gown. He's assisted by a Geneva lawyer even more smug than himself. They seem very jovial and friendly together in the corridors but I have an idea that they don't really get along too well.

As on the previous two days we're all back in the courtroom at one thirty. Then they each have their turn. The prosecutor talks about me as though I'm teacher's pet on prize-giving day. It's nice, if silly. One wonders where these intelligent characters who've had rigorous degree courses and so on could pick up such ridiculous notions. I tend to be rather smug myself, but to listen to him I'm way above all the paragons of female virtue. I love my mother, yet unlike him I don't develop a sob in the throat when pronouncing her hallowed name. Father is a good sort too, as I know, and he's done very well, but now he's described as a sort of Rockefeller cum St Francis of Assissi. Let's not exaggerate!

Only Maurice gets what's coming to him. Even mother at her worst never trotted out half the clichés spouted by the prosecutor. Maurice seems not to give a damn. I understand him. None of this is serious.

The defence is another matter altogether. Just as well I know nothing about trials or the process of law: I'm quite certain that the leading counsel, the Parisian, doesn't believe a word he's saying. He begins by swearing to all and sundry that Maurice is innocent, but after that goes on to explain that if by chance Maurice *were* guilty, it would be through no fault of his own. Maybe I'm a bit slow, but I don't think things look so good for Maurice. Counsel also speaks well of father, mother, Suzanne and myself, though each time he adds some little comment implying that all of us were hostile towards Maurice. According to him, Suzanne isn't normal either: he suggests that Suzanne and Maurice weren't too happy in bed. I know this angle is rubbish because I saw them together and now at last I can admit that it was the very thing I found unforgivable.

He concludes that if Maurice did something to me, this wasn't a gesture of aggression but a sort of protest because everyone had teamed up against him. Finally he talks at length about Maurice's nervous strain and overwork.

With the best will in the world, I've never seen Maurice overworked. He has such a lackadaisical manner of working that mother teases him endlessly. It's true, he does take things easy, explaining to us that he has his clientele. The proof of this is, he makes a good living. But overwork, no. I'm far from being the only one of this opinion . . . I note the reactions of the prosecutor, who raises his eyes heavenwards. The jurors don't seem any more convinced than he is.

The Swiss lawyer takes his turn and launches into a far less idiotic argument. Under normal circumstances, he'd be convincing. Basically he tells the truth. He's the only one to do so throughout this entire trial. What he dwells upon is very simple: no one saw anything. They heard me scream; they saw Maurice covered in scratches and bleeding, but no one was actually there; and thus if Maurice is found guilty it will be on assumptions and suspicions but definitely not via the burden of proof.

'Name a single witness,' he cries, 'just one, and then, ladies and gentlemen of the jury, I'll say to you, *Condemn this man.* But in our law you know as well as I that everyone is innocent until proven guilty. Formal proof of my client's guilt has not in my opinion been established. Thus if there is any lingering doubt in your minds, however slight, it only remains for you to find the defendant not guilty.'

At least that's the gist of what he says. But it must be admitted that nobody is impressed. I see from people's expressions that in their view Maurice is guilty.

Mother feels obliged to come over to me, put her arms around me and kiss me. I watch a woman in the jury who from time to time has been staring at me as if I'm a fledgling fallen from the nest: she is now wiping a tear from the corner of one eye and making much of the mopping up operation.

'Before the court adjourns while the jury retires,' says the judge after the defence summing up, 'I call upon the accused to be upstanding. Have you anything you wish to add?'

Maurice stands up again and looks at the judge and the public prosecutor. I get the impression that he is doing the judging, judging them both. He turns towards the court itself and us: father, mother, Suzanne, police, experts, all the witnesses.

'If you have something to say, do so now,' the judge repeats impatiently.

Maurice catches my eye. I feel he wants to ask me a question. He looks very gentle, like when he called me his wife, and as if he wants to thank me.

'The jury will now retire to deliberate upon its verdict.

Prisoner in the dock, for the last time, do you have anything to add?'

'Yes, your honour . . .'

'Well . . .'

'I am guilty.'

I scarcely hear him although there aren't that many people in the courtroom and the silence has sometimes seemed overpowering, this small phrase creates another silence, so deep that all other sounds appear to echo endlessly: shoes squeaking, wood cracking, even our own breathing. It all finally stops, except for his voice.

Mother stifles a sob and I feel that everyone there, the assessors and witnesses too are suppressing a cry of astonishment. The silence vibrates anew with questions and doubts that we've all buried in our consciences. The judge and his assessors murmur among themselves; Maurice's defence is engaged in frantic discussion. Maître Jarrot sighs. I alone know . . . What? I know the truth will out. Maurice is smiling. I am not even sure whether anyone else sees his smile. It's a half-smile. His eyelids almost close. His lips do not part.

'Your honour, members of the jury,' he declares, enunciating every word clearly, 'I raped Naomi-Anna, raped Nea. All the charges against me are justified.'

The Parisian and the Swiss turn in unison as if in an operatic duet. They gesture to their client, but Maurice takes no notice of them.

'Your honour . . .' the French counsel begins.

'No, Maître, the defence summing up has been completed. As required of me in Criminal Law, I have given the accused an opportunity to speak, so let him do so . . . Continue, sir . . .'

'. . . yet what you think you know,' Maurice goes on deliberately, 'is nothing compared to what actually happened . . .'

He speaks very quietly as though it's enough if he himself can hear: he seems to be addressing no one else. He looks up

113

again, and this time a real smile lights up his face, a fine smile . . .

'I've always loved Nea. Nea is the only woman, the only human being I've ever met. I was crazy, I didn't realize, I lied to myself. I'd help her with her homework and tell her not to slouch, just like her parents did. Nea is a woman. I don't think I've ever met a real man or woman in my life, before her. I only met play-actors, like myself, and men who became trapped in their roles and attitudes, who talked nonsense, knew nothing and wanted nothing. Nea knows more about that than you or anyone else in this room. She understands what desire, will and pleasure mean . . .'

'I will not allow you to utter these obscenities,' the judge says curtly. 'In your mouth the word pleasure, in your victim's presence, is a new outrage, a further crime to add to the one to which you have finally confessed. Proceed, but briefly. You are not here to expatiate or to justify yourself. You have confessed. The court will take this into account in its judgment, but I will not tolerate your abusing the privilege allowed you by law . . .'

I've never been so happy in all my life. I wasn't mistaken, Maurice loves me. He loves only me. Suzanne meant nothing to him . . . Or if she did, she meant something in relation to us, with or between us . . . If she'd wanted, Maurice and I would have loved her. It was she who didn't understand. Nor did they: Maurice was right, they're blind. I'm not though: Maurice is a man, the only man I've ever met. Mother for all her airs and graces didn't see this, nor did father, who thought himself magnanimous and indulgent in letting Suzanne marry Maurice.

'Since I've begun a confession, your honour, do allow me to unburden my conscience,' Maurice continues.

It can't be said that he is being flippant, though he is gazing at the court officials with the mischief of a small boy suggesting to his parents that he hide behind a curtain or under the table.

'Be concise,' says the judge crisply.

114

'My attack on Nea wasn't the first time,' says Maurice staring hard at me. 'Before I even married her sister, I'd taken her virginity ...'

'By force?' demands the judge.

'Of course, your honour, by force. Whether or not one likes it, the penis tears the virgin hymen. I didn't create this violence, nature did ...'

'How dare you invoke nature!' the judge fumes.

'I was confining myself to answering your question, your honour.'

Naturally Maurice used force, *his* force. Before that I'd never suspected there was a pleasure keen and stronger than that my hand gave me, or that there could be an emotion greater than imagining what one likes how one likes. When Maurice penetrated me for the first time, what I loved about it was *not* loving, was being hurt and feeling disturbed. What can't be done alone *is* disturbing, is creating a pleasure one hadn't imagined, discovering a picture never before glimpsed.

'I often forced her to submit to my desire,' Maurice stresses.

'Were you aware she was frightened?' asks the judge.

'I'm saying I imposed my desire on her.'

'And had you no sense of shame at inflicting your lust?'

'Yes, your honour. I couldn't help myself. I tried everything to rid myself of this urge, to escape the hold she had over me ... I used to tell her what to do and she would obey me. Until the day when she made my face bleed and scratched my back ..'

'Because in the end the unfortunate girl, knowing that her parents were in the offing, realized she could rebel, free herself from you ...'

'Because she realized, your honour, that she could seize hold of me as I'd done with her and hand me over to everyone, so I'd be even more securely hers ... The proof of it is that today, deep in my heart, I only have love for her. I feel only love towards her and I thank her.'

115

'You profane the word love. Perhaps that is the gravest of all crimes,' the judge thundered.

The man who has previously been so calm erupts into a real rage. A rage I find very impressive too, very honest, yet less fine and honest than the lies and the love of Maurice.

The judge leans over to each of his four assessors one by one and then says:

'Prisoner in the dock, be seated. In the light of declarations made by the accused, which as far as this court is concerned constitute new factors in this case, I ask, by virtue of the powers vested in me, that the victim of this atrocious crime be recalled to the witness stand. I must apologize to her parents. I hope that she herself appreciates that the gravity of the maltreatment she has received obliges this court to go on seeking the whole truth for as long as necessary. The court must, after due and proper deliberation, reach a fair yet precise verdict upon the crime committed and its alleged perpetrator.'

At a signal from the judge an official comes towards me but I don't wait for him and go into the witness box of my own accord. I can't wait to reply to Maurice.

'Mademoiselle, do you confirm the accused's confession?' the judge asks me.

'Yes, your honour. We did everything he told you: he would ask me to touch him, caress him, undress him, take off his jacket, shirt, shoes, trousers, socks and, when he was naked in front of me I would kneel down. He would tell me to kiss his . . . prick. I used to do so. His prick would become big and hard. I could hardly keep it in my mouth, but I managed to. He would ask me to stroke his back and buttocks and stomach. I would kiss his eyes and mouth and then he would make me lie down. He used to stand over me, holding his prick with both hands and spraying me with liquid. He used to make me sit in a chair and spread open my legs and kiss my . . . cunt and squeeze my breasts . . .'

'And you didn't resist!' exclaims the judge. 'You accepted such vileness!'

'I did.'

'Did it never occur to you to talk to your parents and complain to them about it?'

'No.'

'Why not?'

'Maurice was my sister's fiancé. A man. I'm only a girl.'

I look at Maurice. I take great care not to smile, for I realize exactly how a smile will be interpreted. But I try to show him how happy I am. I feel as if I'm shiny and gleaming like a star. I'd like him to know. I hope he likes what I'm saying. I want to offer him lies as lovely as his, and as true . . .

'Do you admit these acts?' the judge asks Maurice.

'She it is who must be believed,' Maurice answers, slowly lingering on every word.

We don't stop looking at each other. We both know that at last we are telling the truth.

'Why, when you'd been submissive and silent for many long months, Mademoiselle, did you suddenly revolt against the advances of your seducer?'

'I had to scream, I had to scratch him, your honour. I screamed and scratched Maurice's face and hurt his back . . . I could do nothing else.'

'What do you say to that?' asks the judge, turning once again to Maurice.

'She is right, your honour. She had no other way out. I was blind. She gave me back my sight. My life no longer made any sense and she gave it some.'

'Are you telling me you wish to be punished?' asks the judge sceptically.

'She must have reawoken me and given me back my life, for I was no longer a person any more. Now, thanks to Nea, I am a man for ever . . .'

I sense that the judge no longer understands. He goes on asking Maurice questions. He has forgotten me. I'm still in the witness box but he doesn't even send me back to my seat. He asks question after question and Maurice replies. But while answering the judge, he is addressing me. The

117

others don't realize because he is quite motionless and his round eyes appear to flicker. One may assume that the judge's questions are worrying him, but I know he is awaiting a last message from me, one last act.

My cape protects me like a tent, within which I am concealed. My eyes are a submarine's periscope. My eyes are telling him what is beneath my cape: my tense body, my erect hardened nipples, my taut firm belly, my spread flexed legs and my hands resting at the base of my pubis, my fingers like electric points ready to spark into action. And I can go still further: I'm going to offer him my orgasm, now, in front of all these people. Slowly my right hand slides below my skirt. I raise it. No one can see anything. I stand there immobile in my brown cape. Behind me I hear a voice, it must be Monsieur Banat's, murmuring:

'Look at the poor girl, she doesn't even dare move. You'd think the judge would send her back to her seat. He doesn't give a damn ... They're all the same ... What a swine ... All that needs doing is sentencing him and sending him to prison ...'

With my left hand I keep my skirt bunched up and gently tug down the elastic of my knickers. My right hand slips between the nylon and the silken pubic hair . . that's it, I sink my forefinger between the lips of my sex and on the clitoris. I keep still while the judge continues speaking. It's obvious the judge hasn't a clue: what can he understand of all this? My hand moves again. I offer my hand to Maurice, and with my hand my eyes, and through my eyes my body, inch by inch, my eyes that are closing, my body that is opening, and always, always, my hand that bobs up and down, faster, harder, without anyone being able to see. My cape doesn't even rustle. That's good, so good ... Maurice! Maurice! It's as if my skull is emptying. Only Maurice's name left, floating. Maurice, Maurice. My pulse quickens. They mustn't see, mustn't know. It's lovely and I am his, completely his, and I'm coming for him, for him in me, for me with him, yes Maurice, I love you . . .

'But your honour I love him,' I say, letting my skirt fall back into place, and bringing my arms out through the side openings of my cape, holding them out towards him, 'I love him,' (turning to the lawyers and extending towards them my right hand to which there still clings the moistness and odour of my sex), 'and Maurice hasn't done anything, he told you so, it was me . . .'

Everyone seems to be talking at once. Professor Jungsfeld's assistant leaves her own seat and comes over to fetch me. I don't see her at first for I have my back to her, but here she is beside me. She takes my arm and leads me back to my seat. Everybody is on their feet: father, mother, everybody around me.

'Witness and her companion are now excused,' the judge declares.

But I don't want to leave, I struggle. They pull me towards the exit as I hear the judge announcing:

'The jury will now withdraw to consider its verdict and the Court is adjourned.'

They've left me in my room.

The stupid fat female is sitting in an armchair near my bed, upon which she has made me lie down. The chalet door opens. I want to get up.

'Stay in bed, Mademoiselle, you've had a sedative so you'll soon go to sleep.'

'I only want to go to the bathroom.'

'Be quick then. You're worn out, you must sleep.'

I enter the bathroom, lock the door adjoining the bedroom and open the landing door. As I thought, my parents have just come back, they are in the main room downstairs, talking quietly.

'I'll never get over it,' mother is saying. 'Ten years prison . . . why didn't they *kill* that monster?'

I cross the bathroom, sneak back into my room and into bed. I shut my eyes and think about Maurice. I am happy.

Chapter VII

THE DIRECTRESS

Go, absolve yourself of the crime of which you speak.

Sophocles: *Oedipus the King*

Immediately the trial ended, we returned to Paris. Life went on as before. Suzanne did not return home. At first she stayed in an hotel because she did not want to see the flat she'd shared with Maurice again, and on father's advice she set off on a long trip abroad. This narrowed itself down to a journey to Italy and then, much to our surprise, after stopping off in Milan for two months she wrote to us to say that her health did not allow her to travel any further. Her health and a handsome Italian industrialist who had set her up in a flat and of whose existence we learned a year later. He was a married man, and since divorce isn't recognized in Italy . . .

I changed *lycée* so as to avoid scandal, but soon got back to my habit of being undisputed top of the class. My life was divided between work and masturbation. There was no room for anything else. I've always masturbated and always enjoyed it. In spite of the catechism and various devious remarks from my mother, I've never been ashamed of it, but would, in a way, masturbate with indifference. Maurice's arrival on the scene had developed and complicated my attitude towards this pleasure. Yet it was while caressing myself in the courtroom in front of Maurice, who guessed everything, under the eyes of judge and jurors who saw nothing, that I reached the paroxysm one always pursues but rarely attains.

Orgasm is no longer enough for me. I must pave the way so that, after climax, I am struck down like a tree under the axe. When I've come properly I feel so fragile that it seems to me momentarily that the slightest movement could break me for good. Then life flows back like a freshwater spring, thirst-quenching, and everything takes on a new value – colours, sounds, smells. So orgasm enfolds all. When I am insatiable I start again and there the real difficulties are encountered.

That dryness prior to the second orgasm I at once seek cannot be ignored. Every time I invent new methods, pursuing these as long as necessary. I know myself so well that I always manage to reach a trance-like state. The moment my mind isn't set on some work, lessons, or reading, I prepare myself. Anyhow reading – and this is why I mention it – builds a bridge between work and my search for pleasure. Books create a no man's land between the two, an amorphous zone into which at first I escape; but escape, like those mazes that always end up leading you back to the very same statue at their centre, carries me towards pleasure.

To me my hand is no longer an implement for work, it's primarily the instrument of my pleasure. Sometimes the mere fact of looking at my palm, then placing it on my bush, gets me to the brink of climax, or again, if I tickle my left wrist with a finger of my right hand, that's it, I'm almost there. I manage to paralyse all the feelings inside myself which could distract me from my pleasure, like those ant-eaters which squirt an anaesthetizing liquid upon their prey before devouring it. But the anaesthetic only affects what is foreign to my pleasure.

As for my vagina, it's not important, nor are my breasts ... my hand, yes ... and especially certain hollows whose contact makes me almost gasp with anticipated pleasure: armpits, groin, those twin dimples just above my buttocks which I can feel under my hands when standing very erect in front of my mirror. My neck, ears. I adore my ears, I stroke

121

and tickle them, my fingers lick at them. I use my lips and tongue too and my teeth, of course. The problem is, though, exactly how to use each part of my body and the precise moment when to bring one part or another into play.

Since the trial I can no longer dispense with Maurice during these masturbatory fantasies I'm relating. Yet Maurice by himself is never enough for me. My main successes evolve from situations in which Maurice is associated with another. The existence of this other need not be any too clearly defined. This other element may be a reflection, a person talking, a cat crossing the room and purring amorously; it need only be an hotel chambermaid's legs under their little black skirt, or the door to an apartment block in the Rue Paul Valéry which, according to classmate's revelations, is a brothel.

Right on cue, Maurice appears on the scene: his own role is always more brutal and much less complicated. Sometimes he arrives fully dressed, sometimes stark naked. If dressed, he undoes his zip and his rigid sex – I think of it as a prick, not a sex – is very close as he forces me, fully dressed as I am, to kneel down. I never wear any panties because he has forbidden me to do so. He lifts my skirt, or if I am in slacks makes me lower them. Then I must crouch on the ground without looking at him and he takes me from behind, kneeling without touching me.

If he is naked, he faces me. It sometimes happens that he undresses me himself, or else tells me which clothes to take off. The order varies. Sometimes it's my pullover or my blouse, never the brassière, because as with panties, these are forbidden me, nor the skirt. On certain occasions he prefers me to remain fully clothed to the waist, taking off the skirt alone. He moves towards me and takes me in his arms, for instance, placing me gently upon the bed. He tells me to spread my legs and penetrates me like a breath of frosty air. Or again he may thrust himself brutally upon me, parting my thighs with his hands, taking hold of my feet and spreading my legs wide on either side of his body, bearing down with all his weight: his prick never penetrates me as deeply as it does then. I feel as if he will pierce my stomach and emerge through my throat.

In one of my fantasies, he does not touch me. I play with myself for him and he too caresses himself, for me. I come twice, once for myself, the next time as though I am he.

The nicest of my scenarios is one of fatigue, lassitude: I am exhausted, sated, have come – too much, and am sure I'll never come again. He is lying beside me naked, not as a man but as a baby, his skin very smooth, very soft, far softer than mine, while his sex is not erect. It is very small, tender, fragile in the nest of its testicles and curly hair, so frail, so round and soft . . . I touch it, play with it trying to coax an erection, but do not succeed. I love this fragility, this impotence. I say to him: 'My impotent one, my impotent.' This word is as sweet as 'birth', as disturbing as 'climax'. We're both of us newborn, scarcely in existence, playing in the lap of our naked mother, my sex merging with his, melting against his bush. Around us are confused noises: a chair grating along the floor, a squeaky door, the soft hiss of table castors, and then his infant's genitals suddenly swell up like the smoke that turns into a genie from an enchanted bottle. That's exactly how it happens. These aren't symbols re-created after the event in order to explain what I was and how I used to think. Everything takes place as I describe it.

Do you know what a tiny male sex is like, when it's soft and round and can never, never grow larger, and which one would like to keep cupped in one's hands? I put my mouth over it, cover it with little kisses, butterfly kisses, teasing kisses, languorous kisses – and here it is, enlarging, growing rigid, while I am growing moist because it is erecting inside my mouth which is a sex. I don't need to touch my cunt any more, for it is so liquid that by pressing together my thighs, crossing my legs, gently and almost imperceptibly moving my hips, the clitoris seems to rub against itself, of its own

123

accord, like his prick within my mouth. Is my clitoris a prick inside his mouth or his prick a tongue in mine? We swell together, are born together, together become giants, marvellous Cyclopses borne aloft, in a castle in the air . . .

Of course I can't go on indefinitely like this, feeding my amorous fantasies with a Maurice who is each day fading from my memory. Luckily he finds a way of sending me a letter. One morning at the *lycée* door, a furtive-looking character slips me an envelope, and before I have time to ask him what it's all about, he disappears. I open it and read:

Nea,
You gave yourself to me and I took you. In love, only what in false is criminal: our confessions, by contrast, were true. My prick and your cunt were only united thanks to you. Playing the pupil, you became my mistress in every sense – that is to say, my love and teacher. You showed me the evidence of love, and I await further lessons from you. I'm lucky enough to be alone in my cell, so I can dream of you in complete peace . . .
The man bringing you this letter will return tomorrow at the same time to collect your answer. This way we should be able to correspond more or less regularly. Apologies for rounding off this first note which I'd like never to end, but my postman is waiting and I can think of no better way of expressing my love for you than masturbating for you before signing this

Maurice

My reply is simple: we merely exchange our dreams, as we did on the last day of the trial. Thanks to our letters, we are never separated. Maurice writes that he masturbates frequently, identifying with me so closely that sometimes he feels I too must be coming in unison with his hand-movements, wherever I happen to be at that particular moment . . . We do not work out any particular code between ourselves nor do we set up rules, but our letters never discuss anything except us and our love. Maurice does not describe his prison life to me any more than I talk to him about my studies or parents. If he mentions other prisoners, or I refer to any particular encounters, it's only in connection with our love, for purposes of stimulus or comparison and so on. We very rapidly decided that exclusive possession and what in conventional terms is called fidelity, castrates love.

Maurice strongly encourages me not to limit my amorous and sexual activity to masturbation. Not that he has any worry about the old wives' tale that excessive indulgence in this area might harm me, but so as to extend the field of our pleasures.

For instance, when telling him about how I made love with Suzanne before their marriage, then with Jean-Marc, I suggest to him an erotic encounter with a prisoner. Without actually refusing, he baulks at this. Though he is quite unprejudiced, he writes, he feels no homosexual leanings. Also, he adds, none of his prison companions is attractive. I, however, am not a masturbatrix for nothing. One of the virtues of masturbation is to maintain the passion for discovery and novelty. I go on about it, with such precise instructions that Maurice finally announces to me that he has begun an affair with a young thief.

The choice of a thief strikes me as particularly happy. Like it or not, the idea of abduction is closely linked in our subconscious with that of love. Maurice's thief, an immigrant Spanish labourer, is called Ramon. They have passed each other notes, have held hands in the refectory, have kissed in the showers. Maurice offers me the sumptuous image of Ramon's prick and the taste of Ramon's sperm in his mouth.

That's not enough for me. I then ask them to bugger each other while fantasizing images of me, to play with one another as if I were to become each of them in turn, to use me as witness, and to offer themselves to me.

125

For my part, I seduce two simpletons – the sort who read Political Sciences, fail their first year exams at College, and go into daddy's firm. Imperceptibly, starting from the three-somes which they as smart young bourgeois so appreciate, I push them towards homosexuality. One of them, Jean-Luc, surrenders to a passion so cruel and jealously possessive that I become disgusted, leaving them to their tormented liaison. Passion for me has always extinguished love. I can't help it: only tenderness excites me.

But this correspondence is too good to last. How could I have been so absentminded as to leave one of Maurice's letters in a school notebook? The fact is, I'm found out – by my Natural Science teacher, a big fat asthmatic, mother of a huge brood, whose armpits smell.

Determined to clear my name, mother and father take the matter up with the Swiss prison authorities, who restrict themselves to disciplinary measures: poor Maurice has to endure two months' solitary confinement for my sake. As for mother, she lavishes all sorts of moral and hygienic advice upon me in outraged tones. The letter in question unequivocally reveals my frequent daily masturbation. When I catch the look on my mother's face, I see there a genuine horror, since a disgusted hatred of pleasure is deep-rooted in our society. I am no longer her daughter, but an untouchable.

A week later I am sent back to Switzerland. A boarding school specializing in what an opulently produced prospectus modestly labels 'difficult cases' is my destination. Neither asylum nor prison, La Clairière Institute is pledged to 'reintroduce your children to the social and emotional reality of which an unresolved conflict situation has temporarily deprived them'. To my great surprise, La Clairière is not only a comfortable, but even a luxurious establishment. Father's wealth allows him to demand nothing but the best, yet this is also a remarkable institution

126

whose Directress makes the strongest possible impression upon me. It's remarkable in that money here has the effect of cancelling out all constraints, whereas in general it does away with some only to create others, more complex and constricting. I've mentioned the Directress: I don't want to name her. In my heart and in this narrative I shall continue to call her the Directress, because to me she's been just that, completely that. She's been the one who directed me. This however she denies, maintaining that I've influenced her. Maybe, yet how could I have influenced her without her guidance? She was appointed Directress of La Clairière the year I arrived. Both of us have often wondered at this co-incidence.

There are thirty inmates at La Clairière: imbeciles, hyperthyroids, nymphomaniacs, would-be suicides – all of them jabbering boisterous, dumb, irritable, touchy, or stupid ... All of them, in fact, rejects, like myself. Professor Jungsfeld it is, of course, who has recommended La Clairière to my parents. I arrive there bristling with bitterness. They deprive me of Maurice's letters, my main sustenance, my reason for living. I hold the Directress responsible at once. Here everyone refers to her in the special tone of voice used in prisons or convents when talking of the mother superior or the governor.

Before I've even opened my mouth the Directress describes my state of mind, without passing comment on it. She neither approves nor disapproves. She skips the usual sermons and briefly outlines the programme at La Clairière: every morning the 'guests' limousine', as it's called, will take me into Montreux where I'll be attending classes at the French School, and I'll be collected at the end of the afternoon. I am to participate in some group activities, as few as possible, she elaborates, since my case is different from those of the majority of La Clairière boarders. Their purpose will be rather to make me aware of other problems besides my own.

'But I don't feel I have problems,' I say curtly.

127

'Others have, that's what I said. After dinner, twice weekly, we will meet for a talk.'

'What if I'm sleepy?'

I try on my most insolent tone.

'Well, you'll sleep then ...'

My rudeness is just a formality, since I find the Directress so beautiful that the prospect of talking to her twice a week seems to me actually the only attraction of the programme she proposes for me.

I'll never tire of the Directress.

If I describe her now, it's only because I wish to. What she is, her status, doesn't enter into our relationship. Our relationship was determined by my will, by chance. No – what she is gives me infinite pleasure. First her beauty: beauty, what one calls beauty of the simplest, most universal kind, is whatever is most personal about someone. The Directress's beauty is like no one else's. This difference defies description, and yet I take delight in trying to describe it.

She is a heavy, voluptuous woman, a fruit at its peak of ripeness. Her chestnut eyes with their steely blue whites and slightly downward slant, apart from being heavily sensuous, seem to challenge you to stare at the rest of her, at this full curvaceous figure of hers: the gravid weight of the sumptuous, rounded yet firm breasts, at her long curving back, her surprisingly slim waist and the solid globes of her callipygous buttocks. Her body is that of an earth mother: ample, fertile, both hard and fluid, opulent yet modest, reassuring yet provocative, soft as well as heavy, but sturdy too – a strong, unnerving femininity. The eye returns to that fabulous face of hers, having lingered upon other bodily charms, and does so with delight, confronted by fine skin, very pale pink lips, exquisitely chiselled, and tiny little pink and transparent ears like shells; by a straight nose that contrasts with the delicate curve of her brow; by the play of light and shade upon a smile that bursts open radiantly and spontaneously to bare dazzling white teeth – a smile whose sensual ecstatic charm, finally, never ceases to enchant me, and gives me the impression (if such a thing be possible) that my very soul is being offered a magic fruit, a nectarine in full bloom . . .

The Directress seems to be an optimist by nature. She sees only one alternative to happiness – compassion, of which, like everything else, she seems to have been endowed with more than her fair share. She is, in her goodness, almost naïve. The most astonishing aspect of her character, immediately evident to me, is a sort of inexperience. Like myself the Directress has been a successful student: a Bavarian school followed by medicine at Frankfurt (she is actually German, of Huguenot origin), and training in the most modern psychiatric hospital in Westphalia. Daily contact with mental disorder has bred in her only a marvellous capacity for overcoming suffering through intelligence and this abundent compassion I have mentioned.

Maurice, through sacrificing his freedom for our love, has already freed me from every repressive feeling and all those fears which taboos inflict upon us during our childhood. Thanks to him I have discovered the liberating primacy of pleasure. The Directress, I sense, can help me progress even further, and as with Maurice, this will only be possible, paradoxically, if I am the teacher. So from the start I submit to all the rules, fulfilling all the duties expected of me, and my punctilious docility causes some surprise among the staff.

'Nea, I must talk to you about your mother,' the Directress says to me one morning in her office.

'Why my mother? What does she want?'

'Don't be brusque, Nea, you'll regret it.'

'What's it about?'

'I have to tell you that . . .'

I understand. Mother has died.

The Directress wished to stop me voicing a resentment for which there was no longer any need. Poor mother, she hated everything about me, yet she loved me too...

I realize too late that I also loved her, despite her condemnations and fears. Strangely, I feel that by her death mother is offering me rebirth, a new life... The Directress is watching me: she consoles me by mentioning my father's new loneliness, urging me not to wait until he too dies before realizing how much I in fact love him...

'But he's never thought very much of me,' I say to her with involuntary rancour.

'At this moment each of you is living through a very solitary adventure. You hurt him as you did your mother, hurt his feelings and beliefs through your scandalous and incomprehensible behaviour. Don't you think your mother's death may help him see your point of view and vice versa?'

I no longer know. Yet the Directress's every word is an appeasement, her every look cauterizes a wound, gives me some new direction to follow.

Although she helps me during the next few weeks, I keep wondering how she, who knows just what to say to others, sees herself. I am to discover that she doesn't really know, and that this lack of self-knowledge isolates her not from others but from a happiness that is her due: it is the subtle, almost imperceptible form that her unhappiness takes. For I am sure the Directress *is* unhappy, and I try to find out by attacking her ideas. She is a psychiatrist, and something tells me that her science cuts her off from reality quite as much as clichés and taboos do most people, that like them she forbids herself real satisfaction. During our conversations I discover that despite her professional understanding of what she continues to call my problems, I have the power to shock her.

My masturbation is one of the main subjects of these conversations, because this is the basis for my parents' decision to send me to La Clairière. The Directress refers to it without the least hint of disapproval. Neither the tone of her voice nor her wonderful smile change when exploring this shadowy region with me. For my part I answer without provocation, content to explain myself clearly. We do, however, reach a sort of amused complicity. One day I comment to her jokingly:

'If I were to write a treatise on it, I even have a title for it — *On Frequent Masturbation* ... I'd appeal to authentic sexuality in the way good Jansenists by "frequent communion" quote revealed truth.'

'But the Jansenists, dear Nea, paid dearly for their fidelity to Holy Writ. Like all minorities they were persecuted.'

'So what? It's true that pleasure is openly advocated only by a minority, but one must believe that it pays, all the same. It's worth the high price one pays for it, don't you think?'

'Perhaps you're right, Nea, but if one is able to live outside accepted conventions, I believe it's dangerous to fight them all.'

'But, Madame, I still think we each have the right within every civilization to build our own. Towns, after all, are comprised of houses ... Could you explain to me why my house of pleasures would be uglier than the temples of mammon or of hypocrisy? The day I leave La Clairière, would you refuse to come to my home if I told you that only fun and frankness were allowed under my roof and that there one made love with the doors open?'

'Do you think you have the power to decide everything, Nea? You deem yourself strong enough to refuse all solidarity? Whether you like it or not, you are dependent upon the ideas, even the false ones, of your race ...'

I tell the Directress that this last argument seems a weak one, and she agrees. Since this conversation, she's been teasing me gently, calling me Candide. I'm grateful for her banter, but she does lead me back always to my eternal 'problems'.

'Everything is a problem, Madame,' I say to her one day. 'Living and eating are problems, maybe not sleeping, since sleep can overcome you without your really choosing, but one still manages. As for love, that's no more of a problem than food. The problem is the quest for food, the conquest of love and how to keep it. And are you telling me that the men and women around us work everything out all right in the long run?'

'No,' the Directress admits quietly, 'I don't think so. Ignorance and fear are and will always remain unacceptable. But one must tolerate the existence of those who advance towards pleasure with a less assured tread than your own.'

'But why? To tolerate error in this field is being a party to it! What do you do here with each one of us? Do you tolerate our illness in order to cure us of it? No. Through intolerance of the unhappiness of these thirty or so rich kids in your charge, your life would become intolerable to you. Take care.'

I've scored a point. From now on the Directress shows a kind of shyness towards me. My accusation of altruism really hit home. I love these arguments that give me, first, the rather vain pleasure of juggling with generalities and the subtler one of shooting arrows at random and sometimes finding that I've hit the bull's-eye.

'Are you criticizing my masturbation, yes or no?'

'I condemn nothing, Nea. I'm only telling you that people who do condemn have just as much right to respect as you ...'

'But I'm not condemning them. I pity them. Anyway, do *you* masturbate?'

'I have no intention of answering you, Nea. That would be leading our conversation into a dead end.'

'Why is that?'

'Because I'm a doctor. I subscribe to medical ethics. If I introduce a personal element into our relationship, I'd be exceeding my function.'

132

'Because you prefer being impersonal with me,' I say teasingly.

'Nea, how can you say that? You know very well that I ...'

It's true, I do know. The Directress has a soft spot for me. To be quite honest, it's not surprising, for I'm far and away the most normal of the lot here, and much the most attractive. As for intelligence, I've never hidden the fact that nature gave me plenty. Yet this last exchange helps me understand something else: I can move the Directress. I can shock her, worry her and touch her feelings too.

Going on from there, I have another thought: if I can touch her, can't I seduce her? No Machiavellianism behind the word. Rather, a need for conquest: still more so the hope of shattering a solitude that has begun to weigh heavily upon me.

Contrary to the current myth, making love isn't achieving the fusion of two beings. That never happens. Even in the most simultaneous orgasms, sustained by the most absolute love, each of us remains an island. You don't fuse together in love. On the contrary, the truest, greatest, purest love is that which exposes one completely to the other's gaze. To give oneself unreservedly means not only giving one's body, not only sharing in the other's pleasure, but offering the nakedness and wholeness of one's own pleasure with its inmost, darkest secrets.

The ambition that suddenly grips me is this: instead of these college girl quibbles, what I must offer the Directress is the testimony of my truth in the flesh.

Great intelligence and real subtlety are often easier to catch out than common-or-garden astuteness. An ordinary teacher would never have been taken in by my tricks, or would only have gone along with them consciously. Under the pretext of intellectual inquiry, I manage to elaborate daily and in ever more lurid detail, on my amorous constitution and cherished erotic images.

Knowing the Directress's innate shyness and tact, I become more and more brazen towards her every day. I've made some sly changes in the way I look: not only am I making up my lips and eyes but also (she doesn't yet know this) the areolae of my breasts and my navel too. I carefully shave round the edges of my pubis to emphasize the crisp shape of the little silken triangle, and I pumice the skin on my elbows and the soles of my feet until it's as smooth as that on my stomach. I have my hair cut very short, which makes me look boyish and yet vulnerable. Suddenly my breasts seem all the more rounded as a result. I've not worn a bra for years, but I did go back to wearing knickers. I stop doing so. Which is quite difficult, since I'm now wearing so little that I must be extra careful in all my movements, so as not to expose my nudity too soon and to others, rather than to the one to whom I want to offer it.

I'm sure that it's through not wearing panties and painting my breasts that I've plucked up the courage to go so far with my plan, so quickly. A prude would say a devil is possessing me. The Directress laughingly admits that she can no longer recognize this merry imp – an imp, moreover, who thinks only about tormenting her.

My eyes and lips gleam – oh, I'm sure of it – gleam with desire. The Directress's mixture of trimness and voluptuousness, her body's heavy curves and its milky lightness, fill me with flickering lusts, wild desires which I transmute to childish giggles and coltish gestures.

One evening, as if unthinking, I kiss her on both cheeks when I arrive. She's caught unawares and from then on it becomes a ritual. I also kiss her before going to bed, then I change another of our habits. I've usually sat in the big armchair while she sits on a settee where she can lie full length and stretch her legs while listening to me. She may not know, but I do, how it happened that one fine evening I find

134

myself sitting next to her, her legs between me and the back of the settee.

And thanks to that happy spontaneity which is so easy to affect when one is in the throes of a strong desire, one evening I slip my hands into hers, my head against the hollow of her shoulder, while I talk, talk about nothing in particular.

I've also invented a phobia, which though I've made it up has gradually become so real to me that I often see the Directress's face cloud over as she gets worried. Round about ten thirty or eleven at night it starts, at about the time I'm supposed to be getting ready for bed: I'm frightened, I have nightmares. I can't sleep. An indefinable anguish seizes me. The reason for it? I don't know: it creeps up on me, eats into me like an acid.

The doctor at La Clairière is consulted and prescribes me some tranquillizers which I flush down the toilet. The Directress is observing me, sounding me out, trying to fathom the cause of this new illness. She's the reason, she's the cause, my darling Directress whom I desire so very much. This desire torments me, prevents my sleeping, frightens me – yes, I really am frightened. It's not hard to look at her through eyes filled with distress. Distress at not having her to myself, at not being hers. What anguish, horror, injustice!

'No, I swear to you, I can't go to bed now, it's impossible, I just can't ...'

Suddenly it's true, I cannot leave her. I feel that if I leave her tonight I'll go mad. She believes me and she's right. We spend together the most amazing night of my life.

She is lying on the settee. I'm very uncomfortable wedged beside her lap. Against my buttocks I feel her pubis like an incandescent glow. She talks to me, reassures me and slowly I bend backwards, thrusting my back against her breasts, my head burrowing against her collar-bone like a young calf seeking its mother's udder, nuzzling. I am trembling with

135

desire, with fear that she won't understand and will push me away. And then suddenly I sense that she has fallen asleep. I recall how Suzanne let me take her by surprise while she slept. But I guess, rightly or wrongly, that if I am to go about things the same way now it may be disastrous: she'll have time to come to, regain control of herself and send me packing, invoke those blasted professional ethics that forbid any intimacy with any of us. She has stressed to me the gravity of such a violation of her Hippocratic oath. I must therefore make my move before she has time to react, speak or understand.

I lean forward and gaze at her: she's worn out, exhausted, her legs dangling. Her breathing is irregular. Her complexion, usually so delicate, is flushed: her eyes are leaden and her cheekbones rather too red. Her forehead and nose seem too shiny. She is less attractive than usual; more thrilling than ever.

With one movement I am naked and kneeling beside her. Very warily I slide both hands beneath her skirt, between her thighs. She doesn't react, doesn't immediately understand. I part her legs and with an unwontedly brutal gesture rip off her panties, most of which come away in my hands, and plunging my face between her legs I crush my mouth violently against her vagina. She tries to get up but can't manage it. The effort to do so has precisely the opposite effect and lays her even more open. I wrap both my arms around her waist and sink deeper into her. I plunge into a lake of lava. It burns, acrid, acid. Good. I re-encounter my own smell and taste, feel my own tensed muscles and her stomach muscles like an elastic wall against my head, and her thighs which in turn are heaving and contracting to try to throw me off, and her hands upon my shoulders struggling to push me away. But I am wrapped round her like a vice, I tear, bite, drink her. She'll hate me, send me away, I'll never see her again. Too bad – I'll have had this happiness.

136

And suddenly I feel everything inside her let go, I know she is responding to me, that she is mine, mine for ever.

Her sex spreads and comes to life under my mouth, and my tongue wriggles like an eel in a pond. I drink and breathe her, gently my lips wander over the lips of this sex which is mine, the darling sex of this darling woman whose hands I can feel resting on my head, their fingers sinking into my hair.

An hour later we are together in her bed. All the lights in her room are on and I am looking at her. My eyes drink her in, just as my mouth has drunk its fill of her, rediscovering the body I'd imagined beneath her clothes, finding once again the skin my fingers had felt in dream.

In June I return to France to take my *baccalauréat* exam, which I pass with flying colours. My father isn't in Paris. Aunt Lucette welcomes me home and stays there with me for the three weeks between the written and the oral exams. She tells me with some embarrassment that poor father is very low ... They're worried that it's a nervous breakdown. Under the circumstances, everyone in the family feels I should stay for at least one more year at La Clairière.

On the station platform, the day I return there, the Directress, giving me a long kiss, says:

'Now Nea, Maurice must be released.'

Chapter VIII

THE WOMEN PRISONERS

In order to bring a work into being, I have to be interested in it.
G. W. F. Hegel: *Introduction to the Philosophy of History*

We are the prisoners now, prisoners of our own making, prisoners of a love fed upon ambiguities and phantasmagoria; our love extended to Maurice, exalted by his absence, yet which can never completely blossom without him.

Already he is in our every caress, in the images we exchange, in each of our postures, positions and explorations ... One day this captive Maurice our fantasy frees each night will have to confront the other Maurice who, inside his cell, is inventing a freedom of which we know nothing. Loving each other means loving all our various experiences in all their differences and permutations. If we do not love Maurice when he is, at least, sitting opposite us in reality, as we now love the fantasy Maurice in all his insubstantial ubiquity, it is our love which will be called in question. Everything must contribute to our love ...

Here I pause, because while evoking the ambitions, the risk and the instability of our undertaking, I tremble today just as I used to in the past, with desire and fear. Only an immediate crushing embrace can reassure me. Yes, between this point and the 'I' that follows, I must masturbate, call up through climax the joy and regrets reawakened by these over-elaborate memories, recalling how I always used to have to run into my room, spread my legs, and with my eyes wide open but seeing nothing, conscious of nothing, almost without feeling anything, I would face the window and come, come in order to reassure myself ...

Every liberation is discipline at first. Every liberation forges its chains, conscious of this implied contradiction in our purposes. The Directress and I have only one aim, to dispense with ambiguity by resuming correspondence, somehow, with Maurice. This will be the first step of the imaginary towards the real.

Thus, with a little ingenuity, the correspondence begins again: thanks to a warder, I've been able to send Maurice an initial, very brief letter, relating the circumstances through which we were separated and requesting his own news. I end with our usual farewell catch-phrase, the secret, naïve formula of prisoner to prisoner: 'Me in you in me.'

Maurice's reply a week or so later is not cool but distant. He is very sorry for me, yet his tone isn't warm. He just says he's all right. One reassuring note, he follows my example in ending: 'Me in you in me.'

He wants me to take the initiative in our new way of loving. So my second letter is a long description of the Directress, a detailed account of our pleasures. I end with the phrase: 'She in you in her in me.'

His second letter is far longer even than mine and a little pompous. I like this tender pedantry of Maurice's. It proves to me that I was right: he loves me more than ever. He has multiplied his homosexual experiences, he writes, but not because he finds any special pleasure therein. 'I mean I don't find a *different* pleasure.' It is because that is the only way of getting rid of the atmosphere of jealousy and frustration that pervades the prison.

Whether dealing with screws or barons, jail law is always based on a hierarchy in which, as in animistic societies, violence plays the role of exorcism. Within these societies of initiates, one only rises from the lower to the upper caste by cruel ordeals. Violence meted out and accepted is the basis of the only real order.

Through alternating from a homosexuality directed

139

towards the youngest and weakest of the inmates, as well as the strong ones; through offering love to the fantasizing onanists (those who make love with the women awaiting them on the other side of the prison wall) or those others, the most solitary of all, who reach climax with the stranger they'll never have; and by means of strong-arm tactics or threats – so as not to be labelled with the stereotype of 'queer', 'pederast' or 'closet-queen' – Maurice has known how to win himself a charismatic image among his fellow inmates. He is their father, master, lover. Thus he has substituted for the rule of force that of an egalitarian community far better tolerated by the administration because Maurice has adopted a convincingly obsequious attitude towards the authorities. The chief prison officer and even the governor know that he runs the prison like the dominant male in a group of monkeys or a wolf-pack. They accept this situation all the more readily now that he affects the most abject servility in their presence.

Maurice is delighted with his duplicity. There's only one reason for, and one objective of, this play-acting: to transmit and share his love for Nea and, he adds, 'my love, from now on, for the Directress'. He too ends his letter by changing our good-bye formula: 'You in me in her.'

While the Directress and I marvel at the fact that he's handled his cock so well without emasculating our love, we regret all the more our inability to release Maurice from a game he claims to be in control of but to whose rules he none the less remains subject.

The summer holidays are drawing near and we have not taken one step further forward.

One June afternoon the Directress summons me to her office. She introduces me to a Monsieur Mosse whose downy baldness and almost invisible eyelashes evoke, like his name, an anaemic lichen.

'Monsieur Mosse has brought you an important message from your father ... But it's better that I let him tell you about it himself.'

'Well, Mademoiselle, your father wishes you to have your freedom. I'll spare you the legal details. The main consequences of his decision are immediately to give you most of the rights of an adult, and in particular that of disposing freely of your assets. These assets, appreciable at that, are mainly comprised of two distinct elements: firstly, your late mother's fortune, half of which reverts to yourself, and secondly, a trust your father has set up in your name under Swiss law. French law in fact makes no provision for such a course of action. Your father has considerable business interests outside France – legitimate interests, I hasten to add, and ones officially declared to the French fiscal authorities – well, your father has expressed the wish to make this over in its entirety to you and your sister, while himself living upon a proportion (extremely modest) of the income from the trust, which he deems adequate provision for his needs. The trust's capital is in theory untransferable. However, it has been agreed that with the consent of the trustees, or if you prefer, your father's nominees – the administrators of these monies, who may only be countermanded by virtue of a rather complex procedure – you may transfer up to fifty per cent of the capital. But should your dealings turn out to be ill-advised, your share of the income will of course be reduced in proportion to your losses. Everything has been drafted and we now only require your consent to this arrangement.'

'Why has my father taken this decision? And why hasn't he come and told me about it in person?'

'Your father has instructed me to inform you that he wishes to free you from any ties where he is concerned, not simply material ones but moral obligations alike. "Make it quite clear to my daughter," he said, "that the moment she is free she can forget my existence ..." I imagine that's just a

141

manner of speech,' Monsieur Mosse adds with a forced smile, 'but that is what he said.'

'So what do I have to do?'

'All that's required is to sign the documents I've brought you. I have all the necessary powers of attorney. If Madame here will allow us, we will visit a notary in Montreux tomorrow, and I've made an appointment with the chancellery of your Consulate in Geneva to authorize by law the documents concerning your majority.'

Father, and especially mother, were far richer than I'd imagined. And from now on it will be I who handle this fortune . . .

Yet I don't immediately grasp this aspect of the situation. My first reaction is that father is abandoning me, he is rejecting me, wants nothing more to do with me. I turn to the Directress and say to her:

'Maurice is in prison . . . father doesn't want to see me any more . . . and what about you? I'm going to have to leave you too. I don't imagine I can stay at La Clairière for ever.'

'No, obviously you can't remain at La Clairière,' the Directress admits with a reserve which reminds me of my first interview with her.

What's happening? Is she too thinking of abandoning me?

'Are you going to leave me?'

'No darling, I don't want to leave you, but that's life. I am in charge at La Clairière, that's my profession, my way of making a living . . . You're rich, I'm not . . .'

'If I'm rich, I'm going to make use of my money. If I'm rich, you are too . . .'

'No, Nea, it's not that simple. I'm thirty, you're eighteen — there's no question of your supporting me. You have trustees, your father's set you free, but I guess that he will be kept informed of what you're doing. No, I think it's over . . .'

The Directress, very pale, disappears, leaving me alone in her office. I am stunned. At one fell swoop I've been deprived of everything. What am I going to do with their bloody money? What use is it? You use it to get what you want, don't you? And yet I've lost everything. I no longer have Maurice, father doesn't want to hear my name mentioned, and the Directress is deserting me. I won't accept it, she hasn't the right to leave me like this.

I get up and run after her: she must have gone to her room. I follow her in there. I open the door and see her lying face downward on the bed, her shoulders shaking. She is, she's crying.

'Why are you crying?'

No answer. I throw myself on to the bed beside her and lifting up her head I look into her eyes:

'Don't, please, don't cry ... I'm the one who should be crying. Why do you want to let me go?'

'But I don't want to leave you or let you go, Nea. You don't understand, you little fool ... don't you understand why I'm crying? I can't bear it, but I have to ...'

'Why do you have to? I've got money, haven't I? Yes or no? You're simply going to leave La Clairière.'

For the first time I've employed the intimate form of 'you' when addressing the Directress. She's done so with me for quite a time. I don't know how it happened, but I've always addressed her formally, and then suddenly I've used the singular 'you', perhaps because for the first time I've really understood that she depends on me as much as I do on her.

'I'm crying too, you know ... we can't leave each other. It's La Clairière we must leave ... together.'

We go on for whole days and nights talking in an atmosphere to which we've previously adapted without a thought but which now seems unbearable to us.

La Clairière is a sanatorium. There are timetables: rising, classes, rehabilitation sessions, meals. Everyone knows that the Directress and I have some sort of special relationship. We've been sly enough and hypocritical enough for it to appear normal. It's common knowledge that this last year I've stayed on more from motives of personal convenience than in order to pursue a course of treatment. I find myself almost on a par with the instructors, nurses and social workers at La Clairière. There must have been some gossip behind our backs. However, I'm sure we haven't laid ourselves open to criticism.

Yet all of a sudden we can't stand that either. I want to live with her right away, to sleep in her room and not have to get up as I've grown used to doing, at four or five in the morning so as to get back to my room on the quiet. I'd like ... I would like not to have to leave her for a second. There it is.

It's too hard. But even this difficulty will make my task easier.

The Directress doesn't like this new situation any more than I do. All the same, it's too silly for words: I'm well off enough to buy ten institutions like La Clairière, and this is just what I'll tell her. 'You want a clinic, you want to earn your living, well, I'll buy you a clinic and you can run that, but it'll be my clinic and I'll be your boss, and that's it ...'

'My boss? What a wonderful idea! Nea, my boss! It's true, you *are* my boss ... I'm your pupil, your property, your thing, whatever you like ...'

I've never seen the Directress in such a state.

She suddenly seems so young, made even more attractive, if that's possible, by this idea of submission, abandonment.

'I say your boss, but it's a manner of speaking, I don't give a damn about it. But what with your scruples about money, since you don't want me to give it you, you can earn it.'

I feel that this idea of an establishment she can run really pleases the Directress. But there's still Maurice, and Father too.

Father, Maurice. Maurice, father. No getting away from it. One rotting away in prison, the other not wanting any more to do with me.

Then all at once she gets the idea, the idea of resolving all our problems at a stroke:

'You know, Nea, the one and only person who can get Maurice released is your father. If your father were to intercede on his behalf – the victim's father – that would carry a lot of weight . . .'

'Why didn't I think of it? I've only to tell the truth, say I lied and it was false evidence, and that he's innocent . . .'

'Not that way. They'll never believe *you*. They'll think, oh God knows what – that you want to save him. No, it has to be your father who steps in, your father alone.'

'But he doesn't want to see me any more.'

'*You're* the one who says that. He's given you half his money and all your share of your mother's inheritance, even though he had a life interest on it. That's not the gesture of an enemy. He didn't instruct Monsieur Mosse that he didn't wish to see you, he said that *you* had no need to see *him*, which isn't the same thing at all.'

'Do you think I can write to him?'

'Write and we'll see.'

I do write. Nearly a fortnight elapses before the reply. But it's not a reply. My letter is returned to me inside an old yellow envelope with a note from Martineau. Martineau is father's ex-chauffeur. He writes that he has been hired as caretaker, that father has gone off on a trip.

I'm telling you word for word what he told me, Mademoiselle Nea, he said, You'll look in at the house the day before I'm due back and collect all the mail, the lot, and throw it into the rubbish bin. I don't want to find a single letter waiting for me when I get back, right?

I very nearly threw your letter away with all the others, but I saw the Swiss stamp, and as I knew about La Clairière and so on, I guessed it must be from you, so anyhow I didn't want to throw away the letter. I thought you might be worried. So here it is. Everything is all right here. I'm sending you back your letter because your Dad's a difficult fellow — I don't mean nasty, but he's funny about this sort of thing, isn't he? I'd rather return the letter to you. Anyway, Mademoiselle, here's hoping you are well, as we are, and my wife joins me in sending best wishes. Yours, Martineau.

I have tears in my eyes.

'You see, he doesn't want me.'

'Maybe he didn't think you would write to him, darling. Obviously he's going through a crisis and doesn't want to see anyone ... It's clear he must have returned by now. Your letter from Martineau was sent off about three days ago, so he's arrived back. If you take my advice, you really ought to go there ... You should go and see him.'

'What if he won't accept me, though?'

'Well, then you come back. *I'm* here, I'm not in prison and I want you, want you always.'

'Yes, but your successor at La Clairière is due here in a week's time: where will I find you?'

'That's true. I hadn't thought of that.'

I, on the contrary, suddenly do think about it. The holidays begin in a week. We can go where we like. That's what money is, being able to go where one likes on the spur of the moment ...

'Malta.'

'Malta? What are you talking about?'

'On Malta. You'll leave for there, book in at the best hotel, then wait there for me and I'll join you. We're going to have the most incredible holidays of our lives. We'll stroll about and do anything we fancy ...'

'But why Malta in the first place?'

'Why not? I've always wanted to go to Malta. Apparently it's very flat and there are lovely ruins. I like the name, who knows why, it's like Rhodes, but I far prefer Malta as it's an independent country. I find little independent states like

146

Lichtenstein, San Marino or Monaco rather fascinating –
but all those places are too civilized, too conservative, too
cold. Whereas Malta's a more disreputable and easy-going
sort of place, sunny, more like the Midi. Let's go to
Malta . . .'

'Right, Malta it is. We'll go to Malta.'

At dinner we make all kinds of idiotic puns on the name
and laugh ourselves sick. Malta is the symbol of our ap-
proaching freedom. It's an assurance that whatever happens
we have a refuge, a means of escape. But in mid-joke we feel
the same anxiety. What sort of welcome will my father give
me? Will he want to help us set Maurice free?

Chapter IX

MY CHILD, FATHER, LOVER

Incest was only tolerable by a kind of divine right, between superior beings who needed to perpetuate the line of descent while keeping it very pure.

Donald E. Carr: *The Sexes*

I ring once, twice, a third time. No answer. I wait. Still none. I've kept a key to the house. I open up, catching a familiar smell. But it's not the wholesome household aroma of mother's era, that scent of wax and jam. It's the smell of a school canteen or a cheap hotel. A mixture of kitchen smells, central heating and sweat. I climb the staircase. On the first floor landing the big double glazed window and its stainless steel are grey with filth and dust. The leather seats shaped like animals and the huge brown bearskin spread over the beige carpet are the same. Yet everything has changed. I don't take in the details, at least not at once, but little by little I become aware that this alteration affects only a few things and is more a question of an overall, essential change in that elegant austerity associated with my parents as a couple. A plug missing here, a glass broken there, a window frame that no longer closes, a door jamb whose moulding has come adrift, circles left by glasses or bottles upon French-polished table-tops, a book lying open on a desk for so long that its pages have yellowed through exposure to the sunlight.

How long has that been there on the desk top, open at the same page, and how many months has the fringed velvet cover of that pedestal table lain in a heap on the floor? Isn't father back yet then? I am disgusted. I continue my inspection without knowing where to lay the blame; I wander from room to room, first to Suzanne's room at the end of the corridor. There too everything is the same yet different. The pale blue satin quilted eiderdown is covered with brown stains. The panels of her dressing-table mirror hang askew. Mother's collection of tiny engraved silver Russian caskets is piled higgledy-piggledy on a newspaper, along with bits of blackened wadding as if someone had just given up half-way through cleaning it. And everything is flyblown and dusty. On the ground floor the little green sitting-room is empty. There's only an armchair and its dust sheet under a baroque chandelier in multi-coloured crystal. Two piles of plates are stacked on the carpet in front of one window. I go across. They still bear traces of dried sauce. I put my handbag on the table and pick them up. I push the swing doors leading through to the office. They open and close with a gentle hiss more evocative to me than everything I've just seen. I reach the kitchen the same way, through the second door with spring-hinges. While making for the sink I see that one of the gas rings is lit under a saucepan from which issues a cloud of steam. I go over to it and give a gasp when the steam scalds my hand. I lift the lid, but scald myself again, and let it fall. I hear footsteps and turn round.

It's father.

He has come in through the door of the passage leading to the servants' flat.

'Father, you're here!'

'Ah, it's you,' he says uncertainly.

'Father, I'm so happy . . .'

I run across to kiss him. He lets me, his arms hanging at his sides. He offers one cheek then the other. He's not very clean-shaven and as his beard tends to grow rather unevenly, his cheeks and chin seem grizzled.

'Nea, it's you,' he repeats with amazement.

'Are you annoyed that I've come to see you without letting you know?'

'No, why?'

'I don't know ... Since you told Monsieur Mosse you didn't want to see me any more ...'

'No Nea, I said ... but it's not important. When are you going back?'

'But ... I'm not going back. I thought ...'

'Oh no, you can't stay here ... no ... you wouldn't be comfortable ... You must stay in an hotel if you have things to do in Paris ...'

'I have nothing to do in Paris, father, I came to see *you* ...'

'Ah.'

'Am I disturbing you?'

'No, but I don't know where to put you ...'

'Listen, surely there are enough rooms.'

'Yes, but I'm not sure where the sheets are ...'

'Don't you have anybody to ...'

'No, no one. I don't want anyone bothering me.'

'Where do you sleep though?'

'I've taken Marcelle's room. Marcelle's old room, you know – the ground floor one by the courtyard. It's very peaceful and pleasant, and easier for getting to the kitchen ...'

'What about your study with the divan bed?'

'Yes, but it's too big, you see. No, Marcelle's room is fine for me, really.'

'But who does the housework and the cooking?'

'Oh there's no housework really when one lives on one's own, and I sometimes go to the restaurant or I go next door to the Italian place and buy things from them – they have everything there, cooked meals too, which I can get them to warm up for me ... Oh I'm fine ...'

'That's not much of a life. What's the matter, father?'

150

'Nothing, nothing at all, Nea, I promise you ... it's just simpler, that's all.'

I've never seen him like this before. It's true that he's been something of a recluse for quite a while. He's drifted apart from mother and all of us generally, and then when he retired into his shell I guessed he must have missed the firm and board meetings. But I've heard that his principle business of bathroom supplies (sinks, basins, taps and other fittings) and household appliances had expanded internationally, with factories throughout the world and even in the USA ...

'Do you still run SCR?'

He doesn't seem to understand, so I have to ask him again. Finally, he nods and I continue: 'Do you still play an active part, though? What I mean is, do you go to board meetings or what?'

'Oh, no, I haven't shown up there for two years ... They really don't need me any more ... As founder of the firm I still have a seat on the board, but I ought to resign, I must write to them ...'

'All right, father. I'm going back to the station to pick up my things from the left luggage ... I wasn't sure if ... I'll be back in an hour.'

'Really? As you like ... Wouldn't you rather an hotel?'

'No father, I came to see you. Unless you really don't want me here ...'

'Of course I do.'

He turns on his heel and leaves the room ...

An hour later I am putting my luggage in my room. I go through the kitchen again in order to reach Marcelle's room. I have some difficulty finding it. Of course, it's the third and last door, the maid's room. A naked light-bulb blazes away on the bedside table by the unmade bed. Father is sitting in a large leather armchair, which I recognize is from his office, facing a television in the far corner of the room.

'Father!'

'Yes, Nea, sit down . . . find yourself somewhere . . . on the end of the bed if you like . . . You'll excuse me, my dear, but there's a programme on, you know . . . *Walking Encyclopedia* . . . It's amazing, they've found an extraordinary lad: he's held the record for a week and he's really quick-witted. He could give exact definitions of all the words they set him, except two, but he was helped out by that motor-cycle champion, you know, the trampoline jumper . . . I forget his name . . . I think the last time he managed fifteen metres or was it thirty-five, I'm not sure, but that's not what interests me. He's certainly the best entrant . . . I find I forget things . . .'

My father. This is my father. At six o'clock in the evening, in the middle of July, in a maid's room overlooking a walled courtyard, watching a television quiz game. I can hardly believe it.

He doesn't seem displeased at seeing me. Indifferent, yet not displeased. Is he senile? No, you don't get senile at sixty what? sixty six or seven.

The first two or three days I'm so stunned that I'm tempted to let things slide, like he has done. I make no effort, don't even try to understand exactly what's happened to him, and adapt my behaviour to his. The only difference being that it's now I who go and buy food at the Italian shop. He thinks my menus are marvellous, and has told me three times running:

'Ah this ravioli you've brought is wonderful. I'd never have thought of it, you see. Must remember . . .'

I've cleaned up the kitchen a bit. It's clean, not sparkling, but clean. I haven't touched the other rooms. I try to understand, make conversation. He does answer me, and these replies seem to me unexpectedly gentle. He makes absurd apologies for everything, on the slightest pretext. He con-

152

tinually asks me if I'm all right and whether I want to book into an hotel, yet when I tell him for the hundredth time that leaving him is out of the question, he acquiesces, even admitting:

'I'm glad you're here, Nea ... I hope you won't get bored. I've become so listless. I really don't know why you stay with an old buffer like myself ...'

'Father I *told* you I've come to see you ... You're not as old as all that, and from what I remember you've never been particularly listless, quite the contrary ...'

'In the past yes, perhaps ... before ...'

The third day, I decide that's quite enough. I think I've understood. Maybe I'm mistaken, but I have the feeling that there's probably another way of getting to the root of things ...

Father has always been something of an amateur historian, and perhaps rather more than that. He loves history and is perceptive and knowledgeable about it, not going in for popularized versions but for original research and first-hand material. One of his best friends, Yves Le Gouen, is a well-known mediaevalist ... I've not spoken to him so far about mother, myself or anything, but now I've brought the conversation round to what used to be one of his pet subjects. I no longer remember quite how I broached the topic, but it's the story of Prester John – the old legend of a Christian king across the ocean with whom St Louis or the Pope sought an alliance. It all took place some time between the twelfth and fifteenth centuries, and I ask him a specific question about a series of fifteenth-century voyages.

'Ah yes, you mean Guillen de Covillan, yes it was one of Henry the Navigator's obsessions. There's a superb account of the voyage ... There's an amazing character in it, Benjamin of Tudela – he meets Guillen in Cairo. The poor chap's been searching for four years, from India to Africa to try and find Prester John for his monarch. The learned rabbi only has to inform Guillen of the disappointment with which his failure would be received in Lisbon for Covillan to resume his journey. He is to spend five years at the court of the Negus of Ethiopia, convinced he's at last found Prester John . . .'

Father talks fluently. I know it's an old hobbyhorse of his. But I recognize that voice of old. I recall his passionate enthusiasm, these details drawn from a multitude of sources. It's really him, really father talking. Since this conversation I've regained hope. The next day I pick up the telephone and for the first time in my life realize the liberating power of money: architects and decorators come for my instructions. I simply show them what I want, I don't explain myself, don't put myself out, and refuse compromises until I'm finally satisfied. It's extremely easy. For instance, there are objections to my first requests: one must begin with the plumbing and wiring if the job is to be done properly. That I don't mind, but they'll have to go encroaching upon father's kingdom – Marcelle's old room, the toilets, the kitchen – and so I refuse.

Well, they work out another system, installing the electricity at the far end of the house instead – wires, pipes, and the rest. The same with the bathrooms, which are completely renovated. I firmly reject the furniture and pictures I'm shown. Saying 'No' is wonderful when one takes a step forward with each refusal. I don't even really know how clear my ideas are, don't know which fabric I like, don't know what furniture or colour schemes I prefer, but on the other hand, when I see the actual designs and materials instantly recognize what I don't like.

In three weeks the house is entirely redecorated by teams of workmen working day and night. It hasn't been too big a job. Only the kitchen presented any major problem: I don't know what nonsense I told father, but I turn up one morning at eight in order to take him out for a stroll. He accompanies me remarkably docilely.

We spend the morning in the Bagatelle Rosegardens and

154

have a picnic. After lunch we go for a walk. For the next part I've already had a trial run: I take him to the Victor Hugo Museum in the Place des Vosges. He's always loved Victor Hugo, especially his fantastic side, *The Toilers of the Sea*; *Bug Jargal*, etc ... As soon as we get inside, he galvanizes into action. He knows every drawing and all the editions of the various books. His gestures and the speed with which he walks all remind me of the father of ten years ago. It's a transformation. But it ends the moment we're outside. Once again the slow invalid tread that scares me. I drag him off to the cinema for I am worried that it is still too early to return home. We go to a six p.m. showing, and when we come out I pretend I'm thirsty. I take him to a café on the Champs Elysées and rush to the telephone. The kitchen has been completed, and the cook/housekeeper engaged a week ago, together with the married couple who are to be butler and chambermaid, are at their posts.

'Yes, dinner will be ready at nine. Mademoiselle needn't worry herself.'

I'd like to take her advice, but Mademoiselle does worry herself. I take father back by taxi. When we arrive at Neuilly, instead of going in by the servants' entrance as he now does, I stop in front of the main steps. He hesitates a moment, but he has followed me around since the morning without objections. I sense his astonishment.

Everything is lit up. The simple fact of repainting the entrance has radically altered the appearance of the house.

'This is Julienne, father.'

I introduce our treasure, who has just opened the door and politely replies: 'Good evening, sir.'

Raised eyebrows, but so far no comments. Julienne goes. Father makes as if to follow her towards the kitchen, but I tell him:

'No, father, please!'

And I take him into his old office-cum-study.

I'm rather anxious about this, because I've had such fun

155

here. It's no longer an office, nor is it a bedroom – more, I think, the ideal room for the wealthy misanthrope. I've had a new door put in and have done away with a sort of small annexe whose use I never did understand and turned it into a bathroom. His cheap, pint-sized divan has been replaced by a good and very large bed covered with big chestnut cushions. Everything is in matching maroon, chestnut and tan shades. I've only left him one of his old paintings, a somewhat abstract still life, undemanding and I think consoling. I don't know why I say consoling – maybe because I am waiting for consolation of some sort. Anyhow, I've chosen some books too. Here again I've had some fun because I think father and I share the same tastes in reading matter, which always used to exasperate mother. Father has always doted on what he calls his silly books. But that's an expression of affection, for he loves those books as one does a furry pet: from the Fenouillard Family saga to Lucky Luke, the serial novels from Frédéric Soulié to Ponson du Terrail. But I also know he must have his favourite chroniclers and biographers: his Saint-Simon, L'Estoile's Diary, Boswell ... I think I could reel off by heart a list of the books he'd take along for his desert island. (And aren't I leading him to an island?) There's also a good selection of detective stories in English.

These detective novels are to my mind the biggest test, for it was when father was at his busiest that he'd return exhausted after a business trip somewhere and would devour a good thriller in one evening. Mother, who had been saving up a whole mass of problems and questions about the house, the housekeeping, children's holidays and so on, used to be exasperated by his silent bookworm's absorption.

Father follows me. He comes into the room and looks around with interest, then his eyes meet mine and he asks:

'What's this? What is this, Nea?'

'Your room.'

'But – I was happy where I . . .'

156

'Sorry, father, I haven't shown you the television. There is one. Look.'

I operate the sliding panel behind which the TV is mounted upon a sort of adjustable boom that allows it to be angled towards the bed or facing an armchair placed next to a big bay window that looks out over the chestnut trees in the avenue ...

'Don't you like it?'

Father looks at me again. He draws nearer and stares at me with an unusual fixity. It's not what I'd call his old look: perhaps I might define it as his new expression. It contains all the sadness I've felt in him since my arrival, yet with the lucidity and the depth of his former demeanour. It's as though he has decided if not to revive, at least to react.

'Why are you forcing my hand, Nea?'

'I've left Marcelle's room just as it was, father, with the TV, the big brown chair and your bed. The only difference you'll find should you return is that I've had the whole room thoroughly cleaned because it was a bit fusty. It's just as it was ... Just for you ...'

Father paces up and down and pulls one or two books from the shelves. He chances upon a book he's often told me about, from when I was fifteen or so: *The New Science* by Vico, an eighteenth-century Neapolitan priest, in the Michelet translation.

'Anti-Cartesian, you see,' he's saying to me. 'A man of his time, yet more than a mere man, a man of truths, against imbecile monotheism, the limit rationalism of your Descartes ...'

'He's not *my* Descartes, father ...'

'Vico, the father of scientific man ... That's why he called it *The New Science* ... New science,' says father haltingly, 'I didn't know I still had this edition ... Michelet's translation isn't much good, I'm always telling myself that one day I'll do one ... That'd be nice, a real translation of the *Scienza Nuova* ...'

Slowly he replaces the book upon its shelf. Despite the disillusioned way in which he talks, I sense he is full of curiosity, an amazed curiosity, as though amazed at being still alive, still capable of thought. He goes and sits in the armchair I've put near the window and asks me:

'Switch on the set, would you?'

I adjust the set so he can see it.

'Not bad at all, I must say. The angle is just right. Can you switch off now . . .'

He rises again and opens the door leading into the bathroom.

It is as big as his own room, covered with a thick pile carpet, and with a rocking chair and plexiglass shelving with some magazines on it. He makes straight for the taps, which he examines with a critical eye.

'Heredity!' he announces laughingly.

That's the first bright, ironic smile I've seen from him in years.

'Bronze, eh? I'd never have forgiven you if you'd put in some trashy muck. But we know about taps, don't we? That's what made our fortune . . .'

He returns to his room.

'But you shouldn't have, Nea . . . What's the use? Why drag me away from . . .'

'Drag you away from what?'

'My old den at Malempiat.'

There, that's a phrase he wouldn't have used a few days ago. The Old Den at Malempiat was a phrase used by the Hermit of Poitiers, an unfortunate wretch whose story was told, by André Gide I believe, in a collection of stories, dating from before the Second World War . . . Another book father got me to read, and which had been the occasion for a quarrel with mother, who found it morbid. The Old Den at Malempiat – the refuge in horror, so as to protect oneself from horror . . .

'And why the hell should I have left you in your Old Den at Malempiat, father?'

'I don't know ... It wasn't too bad, you know.'

'I believe you, but *I* thought it was unbearable.'

'You know, Nea, one is always – well, often anyway – unbearable to others ...'

I have the feeling this is an allusion to what I've done, to something I've damaged within himself. But I'm not sure. He looks so gentle as he says it and gazes at me with real tenderness. And then there's a sense of fun, a spark of gaiety which is perhaps the first glimmer of real hope I've seen in his eyes.

'I suppose you want me to settle in here?'

'Of course.'

'Have you seen what an odd looking fellow I am?'

And he pulls me into the bathroom, in front of the winged mirror I've had installed above the marble wash-basin. Standing side by side we're exactly the same height. It's true he looks odd. He who always patronized Savile Row is now wearing some stained old flannel trousers, a wine-red pullover (I wonder where he could have found that) and a clashing green tie with an equally dirty striped shirt. As usual he has gone three or four days without shaving. His beard isn't very thick, but its irregular growth with some bristles still black and others white gives him a swollen, elderly, grubby look.

As I stand next to him I really do look young, and knowing I seem even younger by comparison, I still observe with astonishment that I take after him. We've something in common, I'm not sure what – shape of the head, cheeks, perhaps the tip of the nose. I stare and stare ... and say to him jokingly:

'Do you know you look like me, father?'

'About as much as a chameleon. By being mistaken for you I can protect myself from the aggression of the outside world,' he says with the new irony which delights me.

'Really you do. I've been inspecting you, you have the same gestures and tastes as I do. Take a look at those crime novels I've put over there for you and tell me straight away which one of them you feel like reading tonight. Go on, please tell me now.'

He chooses one.

'Let's see ... Yes, the very one I wanted to take back myself and read this evening ... You see, we're alike.'

'That's natural,' he says, his eyes crinkling with his new-found sense of humour, 'you're a real mother to me, eh?'

'If I'm your mother, then it's your bathtime.'

I take his arm and hustle him along.

'Please get undressed.'

I lean over the bath and turn on the taps. I add his bath oil: I haven't forgotten the brand, *Verbena* by Floris. How many times have I heard him mention trips to London on which, of course, he'd forgotten to stock up with some *Verbena* ... I turn round to see if he's begun undressing. Yes, he's taken off the wine-coloured pullover and undone his tie ...

I leave. Good heavens, I'd forgotten ... I go up to the first floor, into the old bathroom which I've had done up for myself, in order to find the shaving set, those famous gold-engraved razors I so admired when I was little.

I run downstairs, open the bathroom door and wave the set in his face. He is lying in water the bath oil has lightly tinted amber, in that verbain scent that I always associate with him.

'That's so nice,' I can't help commenting.

'You always did like verbena, you little scamp,' he laughs.

It's a splendid laugh, more surprising than the odour of verbena, and it really is the laugh of my childhood days.

And suddenly, because I've heard him laugh like this, because in my ear is this young man's rollicking laugh, I see him. That is, I see his body, a body much younger than his face. The monster – he isn't shaving so as to make himself look older, to feel more of that self-disgust – yet his body is so nice-looking. His flesh has the fragile appearance I associate with an ageing body, but he is muscular still. His

160

stomach is flat – not the slightest paunch; there are a few wrinkles around the neck and the skin has the transparency of age, like the texture of marine flowers. Everything leaves its mark on these too-thin skins. He's a handsome man is my father. And he says I'm his mother. Yes, it's true, I've just brought him into the world.

'You know, father, you're handsome.'

'Disgusting, yes, I haven't even shaved.'

'You are doing it on purpose. You didn't shave so you'd look ugly, admit it . . .'

'There's nothing to admit . . . I have to shave, clear off.'

I go up to my room as quickly as I can. I undress at top speed in three movements, showering so as to be even quicker, and then put on a long polo-necked hostess gown in wool and gold lamé that makes my figure look terrific.

The Directress chose it for me.

I go down again into the kitchen. It smells delicious, the Irish trout is superb and the cook opens the oven to show me the *gigot*.

'Done to a turn, Mademoiselle. So tender it melts off the bone.'

I knock on father's door and he opens up.

'Telepathy,' he says, pointing at my high-necked dress and his own light blue polo-necked sweater. 'Come in.'

He shrugs on the smoking jacket I have placed in his wardrobe along with his suits. It fits him as well as it ever did. He's still got a good figure and now that he's shaved I realize that his hair is far whiter than I'd thought. Because there was that dusty greyness on his cheeks and chin I'd seen his hair also as a dull, colourless mess.

Although he certainly hasn't been near a hairdresser for three months or so, his curly hair is healthy and plentiful and by contrast makes his face look incredibly young.

'You're not just handsome, father, you're stunning,' I tell him, taking his arm. 'I'll show you the menu and you can guess which wines I've laid on.'

161

This too is a game, one of what he calls his educational games.

'Let's see ... Champagne Pol Roger 1967, Clos Vougeot 1929, I won't take any credit for that – I know there's some left in the cellar – and Château Yquem, 1921 ...'

'No, you're wrong. It's Château Yquem, but 1912. You have one bottle of it left, I should think it's the only one, and it must be more valuable than anything else in your cellar. But I thought it was now or never ...'

He eats and drinks and I watch him. I'm not hungry. I eat a few mouthfuls. It's so good to have him here, so nice that he's handsome, so nice that he loves me ... Does he love me?

'Father?'

'Yes, Nea ... of course I love you.'

In spite of my miracles of decoration in the sitting-room I don't want to sit there. I want to go back to father's room with him.

'Make yourself comfortable. I'm going up to change and I'll be back.'

I put on my nightdress, dressing-gown and slippers and return.

He too is in his dressing-gown; he is lying on his bed, propped up by cushions, a cigarette in his mouth. He hasn't smoked one since my return and I've hardly even noticed. Yet without giving it any thought, when putting the finishing touches to his room I have placed a pack of untipped Camels into his desk drawer.

We talk, talk about everything. Mother. Myself. We talk about me without doing so – that is, without our mentioning Maurice specifically, or the rape. We talk about me primarily and later about me in relation to father and how he saw me. An odd scene.

He blames himself for not having shown me that he loved me. He's wrong there, I knew very well he did. On the contrary: I knew it all too well, so it didn't ever interest me. I needed men, and didn't look upon him as a man.

162

I think anyway that I didn't do so because I couldn't accept his attitude towards mother. I couldn't accept his always giving in to her.

'Your mother was a good woman. I loved her, of course. Yet it's true we didn't have much in common, or rather very little. I used to love her efficiency in running the house, her orderly nature, her briskness, tidiness, and her loyalty too. I loved her very much, but we didn't even share our affection for you or Suzanne since we didn't see you in the same light. For instance, I knew you were strong and brave and expected everything from us, all the answers. I knew your demands were limitless. Your mother could only see as far as your school results. She was delighted, she thought you were perfect. That's why she was so much more disillusioned with you than I . . . I mean before sending you to La Clairière.'

That doesn't surprise me at all . . .

It's my turn to talk, to tell him what I used to think of him, how much I loved him, and above all to explain to him the sort of person I am.

'You see, I'm your daughter again,' I say to him. 'And have been since this dinner, since tonight . . . Because from now on I'll never hide anything from you any more. One can't always remain cut in half, only presenting a portion of oneself to others. We're always supposed to be wearing masks, putting on different faces to different people . . . Things don't work out like that in reality. People cut themselves into little pieces and feed you with tasty morsels or they cut off their heads or rip themselves apart . . . Do you understand, father, that I can't, I can only love you totally, with all of myself . . . Or else I must cut myself off completely from everyone, like you did. But why did *you* become so introspective?'

'Because I had nothing left, Nea. Your sister went away. I know she wants nothing to do with you, me or the family. As for you, you were far away in that sort of psychiatric

163

establishment. I also had the feeling that we were getting rid of you, as one shuts away something shameful: it was a sort of amputation, and you too had rejected us, like your sister. At least I was quite happy living like a hobo. I had something to keep me occupied. That den of mine and the quiz-games kept me going. I'd blocked off all the other possibilities and alternatives ...'

'But couldn't you have had ... I don't know ... I mean, couldn't you have got involved with a woman or ...'

'I've always loved women, as you know. I've had plenty of women, but nowadays I can't fancy a woman just like that ... Perhaps it's to do with age, real old age being not wanting or needing a woman at random, only wanting a special, chosen woman – but I didn't have the guts to make a choice ...'

'But you don't have to choose *me*, father. I'm yours ...'

'Yes I have you, Nea, but you aren't ...'

'Don't say that I'm not a woman! I'm only that and that alone. I told you earlier that I'm a woman ... When I saw you just now in your bath and I saw how handsome you are, I knew deep inside myself that I was a woman ...'

I go over to father and sit down close beside him. I rest my head upon his shoulder, he runs his fingers through my hair, strokes my cheek and gives me a kiss. I bury my head into his neck, and in my turn run my hand through his hair and stroke his wonderfully smooth cheek.

'Those cut-throats in your shaving set are great, aren't they, father? Your nice smooth face, just how a man's face should be, in my opinion. All you men can look smooth when you want to. We woman are soft and sweet because we're forced to be. But the more masculine you are the softer you should be able to be and right now, father, you're the most manly male I've ever known or seen.'

I look at him, am thinking just how handsome he is. I slip my hand inside his dressing-gown, against his chest. I feel his heart beating.

'You know I love you, don't you?'

'Yes, Nea,' he says, 'I know.'

'But do you know *how* I do?'

'I'm not sure,' he says.

My mouth is near his face, both my hands are on his face. I gaze into his eyes. I stroke his eyelids, stroke his white eyebrows. My hand slides down his neck and rests upon his shoulders. I open his dressing-gown. He is motionless and he stares at me hard, meeting my own stare.

'I think I know how you love me, Nea. But isn't it this love which has already wrecked everything?'

'On the contrary, doesn't rejection wreck everything?'

He lowers his eyes. He knows very well that his body is accepting, craving what I am daring to offer him. I have to reconcile him to himself. I must help him reconcile his past, his memories, the ideas he has about himself and me, with what we are right now, together. So I say to him loudly and distinctly:

'You know, father, incest is just something one wants like everything else.'

He doesn't answer me, nor does he push me away. I hold him tightly and continue:

'Don't talk to me about taboos or purity, don't tell me about the things I've destroyed myself. What *I'm* telling you is that I regret nothing. I don't regret ruining whatever I have ruined in my life. Even Maurice has only been a source of love and truth in my life and I hope and believe I've meant the same to him. What's happened to me in life, you see, is that I've always done what I wanted. I want to love you and want you to love me. I want us to love each other like sunshine, love in broad daylight. I want to marry you and embrace you, and want you to embrace me. I want you to know me completely. What more can I give you? Joy and ecstasy, the language of happiness. If you marry me and take me and you become everything the word "man" means to me do you believe we'd lose anything, or hurt or destroy

165

each other? No, we'd be reunited, we'd be together again, linked, joined together.'

I hold him close to me, undo his dressing-gown cord. I ask him to get up and he rises to his feet. I too stand up. I pull his gown off his shoulders so it falls to the floor. I take off my nightdress and say to him:

'You see and you look and I too see and look. Now let's get quietly and gently into this bed, if you want to.'

We slip into bed together and I huddle against him, pressed against him. Very slowly and carefully we are searching, we are deepening. All I am giving this man, which I give back to childhood and innocence, is happiness and freedom, and these I am taking too. Once again we become consubstantial. We are finally one flesh born of the same flesh.

Chapter X

THE KNIGHTS OF MALTA

The state of excellence is that wherein the play between order and disorder is functional, elastic, inventive, creative.

Edgar Morin: *The lost paradigm: Human Nature*

The weak choose the strong. Children may one day choose their parents. Women always choose their men. The strong exist or impose themselves, they crush. Yet a servitude can be endured, accepted, or better still, used.

The very exercise of the parents' authority frees the children. A woman chooses because she knows herself to be an object of exchange, merchandise or conquest. As for the taboo of taboos, which one constantly finds in all civilizations everywhere, throughout the ages, it's not really upon incest but on freedom of choice, the real autonomy of human beings ... Sweet, reassuring incest expands and prolongs the solitary pursuit of pleasure. The horrible pains of birth are only exorcized by the mother's first kiss. The mouth open anew – after having sucked the milk – to drink the mother's saliva. And the sperm of the brother or father, in its turn spilt into the sex or mouth of a young woman – the sister dispensing life and kisses – floats in delicious waves, spring and estuary, eternity's liquid chain of being. How else could the human community contemplate this magic link which sums up and plunges life first into society then death, than with fascination and terror?

Father would clearly have preferred things between us to stay implied. Why justify an act destined to remain secret?

167

On his account, first and foremost, and for myself. I like words to mirror acts.

Maurice went further still, because through words, by his confession, he metamorphozed violence into love, my lie into truth. And it's because of him above all that I make father not only look at me, but also listen, when we complete a pleasure that has snapped our strength and abolished our prejudices.

'Do you feel different now you've had me? Now that you've made a wife of your daughter? Do you feel worse, more wicked or criminal? Just like that, all of a sudden? Come on! You only need consult a score of books, any amount of laws to reach that worthy conclusion ... You'd believe it, though. I have the feeling that if I just let you be, you'd think that way. I'd never find you hiding out in the maid's room again, but hanging from a beam, I dare say ...'

I don't know why I am being so violent. Yes I do – I know I'm scared, scared of losing those who have shown me what love is, Maurice and the Directress, and of being abandoned by everyone.

And now if I were to lose father it would be worse still, like the deadly relapse into an illness of which one believed oneself cured.

'Why are you playing these games, Nea?' father asks. 'No, actually I don't think I've changed. But the fact remains that I've broken a fundamental law. I can't and won't deny it, especially not to you ...'

'Well, you're wrong, you're not the only one who's broken the law. I have, I alone ... From my point of view, there was never a more voluntary and yet premeditated act. Before even entering this house and confronting you, I promised myself that if you didn't reject me I would take you to bed. It was an obsession. There was a reason for it, and that reason was and is Maurice. Maurice whom I sent to prison on false evidence.'

Father sits up and grips both my shoulders.

'So your mother was right. There's a darkness inside you, something horrible . . .'

'No father, I don't think so: that shadowland of cruelty in which I was floundering was the Hell you both created. You were both the instigators of my crimes. Maurice, like you, thought that he, a full-grown man, had broken the law by sleeping with a young girl. And maybe he had. But that law didn't exist for me. On the contrary, it was when he left me in the lurch like an abandoned child, an orphan although he'd made me his wife, that he raped me. I wanted to punish him for this desertion. Obviously I was wrong. A so-called normal child wouldn't have acted in the way I did, of course. Certainly too this act of daring was the hard blow which helped Maurice rise above himself . . .'

'So was it for Maurice then that you decided just like that, coldly, to seduce your father?'

'Yes . . . or rather no, you must understand me. I've never known greater joy than that I've had, since my arrival in Paris, of leading you back to yourself . . . and to me.

'The first evening when I saw you looking so handsome in your bath, so little changed by time – what joy I had admiring your marvellous penis, the organ from which I sprang! What mystery and magic! Father, it was no longer a question of Maurice: I wanted what I wanted, and I wanted you. But if I'm obliging you to judge me (whom you may think monstrous) and yourself (who you know are not) I am trying to prove our innocence to you.

'Neither you nor Maurice nor I are guilty of anything. Nor is life, nor destiny, nor people. Quite simply, there's no guilt, only love.

'The little girl bent on vengeance, the lying girl, the girl who introduced the dreadful dimension of cruelty and endured the eternal sado-masochistic balancing act of love – yes, *that* girl was to blame. But I repeat, it was you and your morality that reduced her to it.

'What would you have done had I told the truth? I lost

169

my virginity to my sister's fiancé. "I love him, I want to be his, love him only, and if he wants my sister too, give me to him as a second wife ..." What would you have said then? What would you have done? You'd have sent me off to La Clairière at once ... All right, it's true I should never have unjustly accused Maurice. But you it was and people like you, along with Maurice's own complicity, who sent him to jail. I was still only an apprentice, I scarcely knew the rules of your game ... Today, by sleeping with you, through policy as much as love, I wanted to fill you with love, and by making love with you, to tell you the inside story of what happened between Maurice and myself.'

'But why, Nea? Was it really necessary to go this far with me?'

I don't want to reply immediately; again I move closer to father, placing my head on his shoulder. Again I put my arms round his neck and press my body to his and murmur:

'I love you, father, I love you because you're my father, because I've never stopped admiring my father, or cradling him to a slow lullaby that would sicken me with its love and anguish. Father, I love you, I haven't challenged morality to a duel. Frankly I couldn't care less about morality. Maurice and I have found our way, that's the main thing. What I'm asking you now is to help me get him out of prison. You might consider it as your primary duty, even. If you prefer to label me your lying, corrupt daughter, well, you must act in order to exorcize those lies and corruption. But if I'm that daughter you love, and now your wife too, you must serve our shared love.'

'Right, I am ready to assist your love, since you wish me to ...'

'Our love.'

'Our love ... but how?'

'How are we going to free Maurice? Simple. You'll go and find the Court Prosecutor of Bulle district and tell him your story from a father's angle. I've brought with me the diary I kept at La Clairière the first year you sent me there. My whole plot's there in writing, in detail. The law likes written confessions. I reckon with that you ought to be able to get Maurice released.'

Father set off the next day for Fribourg, taking my 'confession' with him.

Malta is as flat as the palm of one's hand. A piece of the African desert studded with Roman ruins, shantytowns, Greek-style houses, banks, boutiques, open markets, wharves and warehouses, all in an indescribable jumble – native squalor tidied up by the British mania for discipline rather than order. It's a curious melting-pot of languages and nationalities, but it suits us.

The Directress likes it. We ride full in the sun on small thoroughbred Arab horses. Which earns us, of course, the nickname of 'the knights of Malta'. Valetta, the capital, surrounded by walls, and the only mamelon on this *tabula rasa*, has all the charm, the heat and the shadows of a mediaeval Mediterranean town. We wander through it for a day or two, looking around, waiting, thinking.

At the end of our first week's stay I receive a letter from father – a long one. He has managed to arrange an appointment with the district Prosecutor. According to the lawyer he has engaged, there are two ways open to us: a re-trial, with all the unpleasantness and uncertainty which that would entail, not to mention the waiting and delays; and proceedings for early release followed by deportation. The criminal record would still remain, but the latter course of action should be far quicker.

Maurice has agreed to see father. I don't know what they said to each other. Father concludes merely by saying that Maurice has changed a lot. Thinner and more good-looking (he writes), and with 'that introspection I observed in some

171

of my fellow POWs when I was in the German prison camp at the start of the war'.

Father ends his letter in his usual manner: 'Affectionate kisses, little Nea, from your loving father.'

I suddenly panic, wondering whether he wants to forget our meeting in Paris, as there's no mention of it. Does he want to deny (as Maurice used to) what happened between us, and to take refuge in age and order, relegating me to childhood and his own fantasies?

I talk about this to the Directress, who doesn't know how to answer me. Why do her kisses suddenly make me feel cold? Why does waiting for Maurice all at once seem unreal, almost unimportant?

I rush to the post office and send father a telegram: 'Ring me this evening at the Golden Lion. I love you. Nea.'

I've refused to talk to the Directress all day. Tired of my ill-humour she has decided to go for a walk on her own. She's gone off to see the Temple of Hal Darxien. She's welcome to it! At seven p.m. the telephone rings. It's father.

'What's the matter, Nea, why the telegram?'

'Because you don't say anything in your letter.'

'What do you mean? I've told you all I know about Maurice ...'

'About Maurice, yes, but what about us ...'

'That's because there's nothing to say about us, Nea ...'

'What do you mean, nothing! It wasn't nothing to you ...'

'Of course not, Nea, it meant everything. But you're right, when I say nothing, I mean there's no need to add anything or say any more, ever. Now things are all absolutely clear. The only thing that hasn't changed, if you like, is sacrifice ... My duty of sacrifice. Yet isn't that true of all love? If I keep silent, Nea, it's only to leave you free.'

'And what if I don't want that freedom?'

'Remember what you told me about Maurice ... You explained to me at some length that he might prefer to stay in prison than rejoin you, even though he loves you. Things aren't that simple ... Rest assured Maurice wants to get out of prison, and my sacrifice doesn't extend to my doing without you – not so long as you want me near you ...'

'Is that true, father?'

'Of course. Who am I to refuse happiness. The alternative to happiness remains the only real alternative – there's no other choice but death ...'

'Why are you talking to me about death, father?'

'No particular reason ... Quite simply, death comes in its own time, and you too should prepare yourself – for your own sake and mine and the Directress's and Maurice's ...'

'But I don't want you to die ...'

'Don't forget that with every death there's an inheritance, hence an enrichment, rebirth. I love you my dear.'

'When will you be back in Paris?'

'I don't know. According to the lawyer, Maître Daumer, it could take one, two, or even three months.'

'What am I going to do for all that time? Do you think I can just wait impassively?'

'You're the only one who knows what you can do, and what you still have to do.'

'But when shall we see each other again, father?'

'As soon as Maurice is free ... I hope we'll all be together again ...'

All together. That, perhaps, is the key. All together, but how?

Father's reticence; the financial puritanism of the Directress, who refuses to let me support her; Maurice's humanitarian scruples that no longer want love reduced to an episode, however fulfilling; and my own crazy ambition always to reconcile, everywhere to re-unite and ally people –

all those elements are finally resolved in one project. The Directress wants a job and to earn her living – right, she'll retain her title, become, literally and metaphorically, this scheme's Directress. I haven't yet felt like telling her about it, though, and have begun my researches alone.

First I had a meeting with a rather odd character – the Director of Tourism, I think – and mentioned to him a plan for creating a sort of holiday club. But I need an island, solitude ... He hears me out, mildly pointing out my youth and the importance of having the requisite funds. When it comes to my age, I just make fun of him in the most adolescent manner possible: I retort that one is as old as one's bank account, which answers his second question.

'But do you realize we're talking in terms of maybe millions of dollars?'

'If you'd said hundreds of millions, sir, you might have succeeded in causing me some embarrassment ...'

I leave him reflecting upon this reply, because after all my affairs don't concern him, but they do intrigue him enough for him to refer me to his old friend Monsieur Michel Masserou, a Lebanese banker who's been established in Malta some years.

Michel Masserou is a Maronite. He listens to what I have to say about the project and immediately broaches the inescapable subject of money:

'How much do you have at your disposal?'

'Isn't that putting the cart before the horse?' I ask him. 'Wouldn't you rather hear more about the nature of my scheme?'

'Very well, I'm listening.'

'Right, I want the site of this camp at Filfla ...'

'But that's just a deserted rock! It doesn't make sense. There's Gomo, Gadso – plenty of admirable sites along the coastline. Why Filfla?'

'Because it *is* deserted and uninhabited, and because there's no anchorage as yet.'

174

'You do realize that you are multiplying all the costs of transportation and construction five or tenfold?'

'Our preliminary plans will be on a fairly modest scale.'

'But I'm not even sure if there's water.'

'Well, we'll have to check that . . . Will you act for me?'

'It's just that Filfla . . . I don't see . . .'

'Of course you'll be needing an advance, some money for your preliminary investigations. How much would you like?'

'Let's see, there'll be boat hire, hydraulics experts, engineers, draughtsmen and designers, legal questions, the survey . . . I'm not sure, maybe ten thousand dollars.'

'Tomorrow you'll have working capital of 20,000 dollars. I want a report on the water situation by next week.'

'Next week! You can't be serious, Mademoiselle!'

'Did you think you'd get twenty thousand when you asked for ten?'

I rise from my chair and head for the door. The Lebanese entrepreneur rushes forward to open it for me. He stops me first, however, to ask:

'Excuse my rudeness, but . . . how old are you, Mademoiselle?'

'Almost nineteen,' I inform him.

'Well, all great empire-builders are young,' he says, smiling.

'And die young,' I reply.

But on the stairs I'm obsessed with the idea of death. It's usually of no special significance, for I always think about death when I'm happy.

175

Chapter XI

THE HEPTANDRIA

Pan, meaning firstly the Almighty ... His primary significance would be hard to define had he not retained the sevenfold pipes, symbol of the seven planets, the seven notes in music, the seven colours and all septenary harmony.

J.–M. Ragon: *On Occult Masonry and Hermetic Initiation.*

We had to drill down for more than two thousand feet in order to find water. But according to the hydraulic engineer we had reached a submarine water-level extending as far as the main island. He maintained there was enough there to supply a whole town. My Lebanese, whom I now call Michel, turned out to be even more typically Lebanese, more businesslike, more ingratiating, wilier and tougher than the most devious Maltese.

I've adopted the system of always paying him a little more than he himself asks, yet never leaving even the smallest transaction entirely in his hands. The Directress checks up on him.

We have formed a company with a Maltese nominal president to comply with legal requirements, and have managed to buy five hundred acres of rocky ground on the south of Filfla. The Directress has found a name for our property: Neanda.

The first letter from Maurice for three months at last informs me:

According to my and your father's lawyers, I may get a remission of sentence during the next sitting of the Special Commission in March. Its decisions come into force thirty days after that.

So maybe we'll see each other again in April. Your father told me you were worried that I might prefer jail to you. If you read that into my letters, it must have been because I didn't know how to express my love to you clearly enough!

Your father told me he found me almost unrecognizable. He too has changed greatly. I think it's you who have changed us all. You or rather that violence within you, which none of us understood at the time and to which, I'm afraid, you aren't yet quite reconciled.

Your father told me of your feelings of remorse where I was concerned. I understand – though in another sense I feel I owe a great deal to you. You taught me how to change: you wanted all or nothing, unity with the very wellsprings of life and destiny. You were barely a woman and already you were willing yourself to become a complete one. You didn't know the meaning of the word love and yet that alone was what you wanted, you couldn't settle for less. You were looking for the most perfect union with another and multiplied that other to fit your needs, guessing that every unity is comprised of many parts, that no relationship is static.

Why else did your impatience drive you to love me and your sister; why do you live with the Directress; why did you reconstruct your father so that he would return to you as if to his mother's womb? You wanted to shatter the enclosures surrounding our secret gardens, which are in fact prison courtyards.

Thanks to the insights I've gained, the experiences I've had, I've been able to manage here well enough. I recognize that all societies are repressive. As far as I'm concerned, only one weapon can undermine or overthrow them – carnal love, that love so close to defecation and death, love which like musk reeks only to perfume you the better. Let's have an orgy of love – the chorus of amorous moans drowning the death rattles, the screams of ecstasy louder than the battle-cries. To preserve love's happy and self-contained isolation we must, paradoxically, offer that love to everyone everywhere, without reservation or restraint.

At last I am holding the charter for Neanda.

Mother's money has been used up on the initial – most costly and least discernible – works. As though reflecting her own life, imperceptibly devoted to father and her children, she has given us the foundations of Neanda. No one will ever see anything of them, but without her nothing would ever have risen from these parched rock formations.

Her money has paid for the water, the soil for planting, the steps cut into the rocks, the concrete blocks of the harbour sunk fifteen fathoms deep, the telephone and electricity cables connecting us with the main island, the emergency generators, the water tower, and the tanks for fuel oil and gas.

I want Neanda to have all the benefits of contemporary technical wizardry and yet if necessary to be self-sufficient without too much hardship. A return to nature without the proper facilities being available would be both short-sighted and impractical . . .

For Neanda's buildings I've had to draw from the trust father set up on my behalf. My trustees have accepted without undue bad grace a plan I've had forethought enough to disguise slightly. The creation of a vast 'Holiday Complex and Leisure Centre' is something these administrators can understand. Like perfect bureaucrats they have stressed the dangers of such a scheme, given an era of political uncertainty and international unrest. I counter by emphasizing that their shrewd financial investments are as much at the mercy of circumstances as my adventurous enterprise.

An expert of their choice had the casting vote, and he has given us the go ahead. Thus they've come to agree that my activities are as rational or as crazy as their own. Calculated in profit terms, my investment on paper looks a better bet than theirs. It has been agreed that the construction of Neanda will be spread over three years.

For the moment our happy island resembles a kibbutz in the Negev desert rather than a tourist paradise, but our prefabs have the proud look of pioneers' cabins in a new world.

The Mediterranean sun and water don't need much time to work their miracles: the oleanders are already in bloom and the fragrance of the carnations is in the air.

Maurice is due to be released on the eighteenth of April.

At my request father arrived on Malta a week earlier. I went by hovercraft to meet him at Marca Scala, the nearest port to Filfla, a good fifteen nautical miles. We went straight to my room.

I call this room the laboratory because I use it as a testing bench. The original model for the Neanda pavilions is to be constructed after some modifications to the plans have been made. The room is mostly of light wood, staff, and plastics, whereas the pavilions will probably be built of more durable materials.

A young Italian architect, Adriano Cercala, is advising me. Naturally Adriano, who is young and good-looking, slept with me the very evening he arrived. I consented only on one condition, though, that the Directress watched over our love rites, and this she did, standing by our disordered couch, both hands working rhythmically within her oiled and glossy fleece, her ecstatic cries matching our own ever-accelerating and delirious moans . . .

Anyhow, Adriano, like many of his contemporaries, has been influenced by patterns and symmetry drawn from nature – hive design, for example. He suggested an octagonal lay-out, but it was I who formulated our final idea of a

179

heptandria. The heptandria, or seventh class in Linnaeus's system, contained heptaphyllous plants and flowers, comprised of seven stamens. This class has since been abandoned by botanists, but we thought it fitting that Neanda re-establish it, since our pavilions will be flowers of sorts, Neanda itself a bouquet, Filfla the vase containing it, Malta its altar or shrine and the Mediterranean its nourishing moisture.

Our system of room-planning, then, is based upon units or clusters of seven, with interconnecting passages and a main area for amenities such as bathrooms, kitchens, dining-halls and so on. My room is a fairly typical one, in that I have a couch (there are no beds at Neanda) which is an enormous round mattress with a fine linen cover, placed in the centre of the living space. The couch is easily big enough to accommodate four persons, there is Japanese tatami matting, and various panels and partition walls that can be slid to and fro and arranged as screens whenever variations upon the basic heptagon shape are required.

In all the rooms the best use is made of the space available: there are hanging cupboards and shelving, folding racks, adaptable and simple furniture, while the baths areas have every possible facility and are easily accessible in each complex, situated only down a corridor leading off every room. There are well laid-out promenade areas and recreation complexes, also a 'services heptandria' made up of offices and the infirmary. All the heptandriae in general, and their rooms in particular, are lit from above and there is a terrace roof system whereby the terraces adjoin each other, following the pattern of the rooms below. Various outside staircases provide easy access from roofs to gardens, a very pleasant arrangement for summer nights. (For those not so socially orientated – any inhabitants of Neanda who have chosen either temporary or permanent solitude – there will also be allowance and space of their own: Neanda's site is large enough to include specialized accommodation for them

180

too, as part of the considerable expansion envisaged for the future.)

So much for architecture and general plans: into one of the attractive little rooms described father has meanwhile moved his things. He has adopted a loincloth. Adriano and I are wearing light cotton djellabas and the Directress, who is rightly proud of her breasts is, like father, wearing only a loincloth.

I am somewhat impatiently awaiting father's decision about us. I've welcomed him with all due respect, giving him absolute priority. On my invitation, the Directress and Adriano have agreed to make love together before the night is out. Under the circumstances, father should be feeling quite at ease.

Father likes to have an evening bath, and when dusk has fallen on Neanda I show him to the bath area. I've filled one of the larger tubs, with verbena-scented water of course, and when he's in the water Adriano and the Directress enter and we all strip naked. We lay out a chaise longue and together give father a rub down when he emerges.

The Directress is kneeling in front of father and kneading his shoulders. Her breasts bob up and down as she does so and both my father and Adriano do not fail to react. The Italian's long rather thin penis rises in excited jerks at the spectacle of the Directress's full round breasts between which run rivulets of perspiration, and obviously the fact that this massage excites her (her nipples are now like thimbles) is trying Adriano's patience. Ever eager to obey my every wish, Adriano pulls her to her feet, one of his hands cupping a breast, the other firmly clutching her luxurious triangle, and they begin to kiss each other passionately. Watching their urgency, father like myself is aroused, and it's all too obvious from the way he has rolled over on his side shielding his own swelling sex, perhaps because of some last vestige of social decorum, that he too cannot wait very much longer.

Without any of us saying a word, the Directress and Adriano head for her room, half stumbling in their haste, arms and mouths locked together; staggering drunkenly along, their lecherous hurried progress to the door is a delightful sight to behold. I take father's hand, tug him to his feet and, smiling, lead him to my own room.

I lie down and wait for him to enter me. He takes me at once, silently, without haste or hesitation. Our lovemaking is brief. I let him come alone. I only want to be a vessel for him. Afterwards he lies beside me, eyes closed. I let him have a short rest, then ask him to caress me.

He scarcely touches me before I feel myself coming. It's not a violent orgasm like those climaxes which make my heart pound just afterwards, but more like a delicious sigh, the culmination of a long wait.

I think the Directress very much wanted to sleep with father. But he didn't want to. They've had a few difficult days getting to know each other. Adriano and I have been worried: we know that the future of Neanda depends upon the outcome of this sort of test. But the Directress too knows what is at stake. She's persisted, has had interminable conversations with father and by the third day we sensed that at last they accepted and understood one another.

The Directress is no longer jealous of him, nor does she want to dominate him. Father has made her understand what he originally told me, that his elderly manner is only due to his inability to pursue and choose new women.

It was different with me, I am the oldest of them all, the first wife in every sense of the word: his original wife, sired by him.

So we await the sixteenth of April, the date on which I have to catch the plane for Geneva via Rome.

I go through every stage from the deepest satisfaction to the most destructive doubt. The heptandria seems so well-protected and yet so well-adjusted to the outside world. The small harbour is functioning. The Maltese personnel seem unperturbed by our behaviour. Adriano, like a good architect and a shrewd man, has established, wherever necessary, frontiers between our way of life and the outside world.

'Nothing remarkable about that,' he says. 'My first important job was designing a Trappist monastery.'

Our problem here is the same: protecting our happiness from the violence and aggression of our era. We've managed to organize things, but haven't I prepared a new prison for Maurice?

I arrive at Fribourg on the evening of the seventeenth. I've hired a car to take me to Maurice's prison – the Cantonal Penitentiary of Belle Chasse, not far from Estavaillier. Maurice will be out at eight thirty tomorrow morning.

I sit in the car, outside the main gate by eight a.m. After I've been there ten minutes a uniformed guard comes and asks me what I'm doing. When I inform him I'm waiting to meet a prisoner, he tells me I can stay and re-enters the prison by a small side door.

Eight thirty, eight forty-five, nine, ten past nine. Through the same side door previously used by the warder emerges Maurice, carrying a small suitcase.

I start the engine and stop the car right in front of him. He looks up and smiles at me. I open the door for him and he tosses his case on the back seat. He gets in beside me and closes the door. I start off. Neither of us speaks. I drive smoothly. I have the feeling he must be more than usually sensitive to bumps, abrupt turns, sudden halts.

This awareness of how cautiously I must proceed gives me a relaxation I don't usually have when driving. I turn my head slightly towards him and smile back briefly. He settles more comfortably into his seat.

I indicate my safety belt and he turns to adjust his.

We reach Geneva. I return the hired car. Maurice gets my case from the boot and I carry his. It's very light. We show our passports to the Airport police and Maurice goes through like any other passenger. I don't know why, but I'd imagined he'd have been singled out and it would all take much longer than usual.

On the plane we only exchange a few words:

'Want some coffee?'

'No thanks very much . . . not now . . .'

'These flight meals are really awful . . . Sorry, what I meant was . . . I suppose . . .'

'Doesn't matter . . .'

The stopover at Rome seems interminable. We have nothing to say to each other . . . nothing that can be said from airport lounge armchairs, with people bustling around on all sides and regular interruptions in the form of loud flight announcements.

We reach Valetta at seven p.m. Luckily the days are already drawing out. For the first time in my life, I've chartered a helicopter to take us straight to Neanda. I haven't mentioned it to Maurice.

'A helicopter! And you say we'll be there in half an hour?'

'Twenty minutes . . . Otherwise we'd have arrived at about midnight or so . . .'

Inside our oval, quite transparent plastic bubble, Maurice looks down and like him I too watch the countryside below us. Only a helicopter gives one the impression of flying by oneself, engineless. We see the whole town lying within its walls and manage to make out some passers by. I even distinguish the red scarf one woman is wearing . . .

Haim, one of Neanda's two chauffeurs, comes to meet us in the Range Rover, on a plateau overlooking the heptandria. On the short and bumpy journey back Haim does not notice the rhythmic bobbing of my head between Maurice's trembling thighs. Neither journey nor act last long, and as I descend from the car I am still licking the last clotting drops of Maurice's jissom from my swollen lips.

On two great silver trays there are all sorts of dishes and drinks I've had prepared. White and red wines, champagne, beer and thermoses full of tea, coffee, iced milk, mandarin and peach juice. I've made two stipulations concerning the food: everything must be small-scale – mouthfuls of this and that, as in canapés; it must also be colourful – greens, yellows and pinks. Shrimps provide the pink, saffron rice the yellow. There are tiny green balls of spinach *à la Ricotta*, and on a circular chafing-dish several highly spiced stews, together with herb broths and chicken.

'Do you want to bathe or eat first?'

Maurice hesitates.

'I think I'd like to eat,' he says.

He takes off his jacket, which I now realize is far too large. He's certainly lost over a stone and a half. He undoes his tie and shirt collar and rolls up his sleeves.

I notice a tattoo encircling his entire right wrist. I take a closer look. It's a chain of three repeated letters: *Neanea-neanea*. Maurice watches me and smiles. It's the second time today he's smiled at me.

'Tattooing was forbidden at Belle Chasse,' he says. 'But we had a lifer there who'd killed a whole family ... A guy from Grisons, I think, who'd wandered about for some years and returned to his own canton to find that a cousin had conned him out of his inheritance. He took him to court, but it dragged on endlessly with no verdict in sight, so one night he went to his cousin's to ask for his land back. Of course the cousin didn't want to give him a thing. So he got out his military rifle – the gun every Swiss is entitled to keep at home – and shot the man, his wife and eldest son. Then he set fire to the whole place and having done his work went along to the *gendarmerie* to give himself up ... He'd learned how to tattoo on Bali. He could tattoo anything – landscapes, naked women, snakes ... he'd done twenty-five years in Belle Chasse and it looks like maybe they'll let him out next year ... He was paid in cigarettes: he had to have

185

his three packets a day. The screws know he does tattoos. I even think two or three of them have had tattoos done by him. Anyhow, they shut their eyes to it ... I bore the wound for about three weeks. One day a screw asked me when I'd had the tattoo done. I pretended it was an old one ... It'd have been easy to check it out on my police record description ... But I told him Nea meant 'beginning' and I'd had it there for years.'

Maurice has been eating while he's been talking. He's eaten a bit of everything, but as I'd thought, not very much of anything. He takes a mouthful in his fingers, spears a piece of meat with his fork, and has drunk only small sips of red wine and vegetable soup.

For me even eating a crumb is out of the question. I've drunk some soup just to keep him company and can only stare at him.

When he's finished, we go through into the bath annexe and I run him a bath while he undresses. He immediately shampoos his hair a few times. Coming out of the water he tells me:

'In prison I always had the feeling my hair was dirty, even after a shower – we had showers once a week – and I never had time to wash it as thoroughly as I'd have liked.'

I watch him as he dries, and offer him a djellaba, a loin-cloth or linen slacks. These he refuses, engulfing himself in a towelling bathrobe.

We return to my room. Maurice lies down on the couch, his head resting on three cushions. I sit down quite close to him, but without our drawing attention to the fact, we are carefully avoiding touching one another.

What is inside us, between us, is so strong that we have to weigh up our slightest movement.

Maurice is happy, he slowly raises his right hand towards me, spreads out its fingers, then very deliberately runs them over his body. It is the gesture of a pontiff. I feel I'm being anointed like a captive queen. Solomon might have used

186

such a gesture with his beloved from the Song of Songs –
Balkis, Queen of Sheba. I shut my eyes. When I reopen
them, Maurice has pulled back the skirts of his bathrobe and
his right hand is holding his erect penis.

I also pull aside the djellaba I've put on while he's been
having his bath. I place my hands on my knees and stroke
my thighs. With my left hand I part the lips of my sex and
place the middle finger of my right upon the clitoris. I'm
very careful to synchronize my movements with Maurice's.
He has often described to me in his letters the way he masturbates. I know that for him slowness is essential, as is the
precision of the images he invokes – he calls them 'episodes'
– which spur him (again in his phrase) to 'deepest orgasm'.
There is, he maintains, a kind of instantaneous orgasm. This
involves the epidermis alone and not the imagination,
and brings on a climax that liberates the organs in the same
way as a chunk of meat assuages the hunger of a wild
beast.

But deepest orgasm first of all demands complete in-
volvement of the whole being. To achieve deepest orgasm,
in his view, one must masturbate. To masturbate is to make
all that is within us vibrate, to bring into play every nerve,
muscle group, cerebral synapse. To masturbate is to fire a
shot in the desert, to explode oneself; it means becoming the
weapon and the bullet, the marksman and the target.

Maurice goes on wanking very slowly and I know he's
suddenly going to speed up. Then things will happen tremen-
dously fast. I follow his movements as closely as possible
and when his hand suddenly starts pumping away, when the
jet of sperm spurts forth, I feel as if it's this which rips the
orgasm from my own cunt like a scream.

Both of us are breathing heavily. Then I get up to fetch a
towel. I wipe him slowly and delicately. When I return from
the bath annexe he has taken off his robe and appears to be
asleep. I find a sheet, cover him with it and lie down beside
him, careful still not to touch him, and stay like that for

187

hours, staring into the night with eyes wide open, listening to him sleep.

I'm woken by his mouth, by his tongue invading my mouth, by his hands crushing me and the weight of his body bearing down on me, and by his prick penetrating me like a drill. I no longer recall which of us finally gasps 'I love you'.

EPILOGUE or THE ORDER OF DISORDER

'Don't you ever disagree? Doesn't anything unpleasant ever happen among the Tasadays, nothing that troubles any of you or all of you?'
'There's nothing that isn't good,' said Balayam.

John Nance: *The Noble Tasadays*

I've been writing about Neanda, but Neanda is another story. It's a story which is beginning. I don't know if it will have an end; perhaps it can't even be written.

The Maltese of Marca Scala call it an Italian word, *manicomio*, madhouse. Maybe the strange bouquet-shaped cluster architecture of the heptandriae, of which there are now over twenty, inspired them ... Or that we're like some strange Order to them – for without having planned to, we've christened ourselves Nouns and Neads. That invites laughter, I know, but names are born like things, they're never anything but the order of disorder, a means of recognition. If we call ourselves Nouns and Neads, this is done in the same spirit as giving precise names to the ropes on a sailing ship, in order to avoid mistakes in handling.

We at Neanda have all had to describe ourselves, define our behaviour. I won't use the word 'ideology' – not that Neanda claims to be above ideologies or that it believes in escaping from systems. Rather, it wants to remain viable within the context of all systems. Human societies have gone through so many changes already, yet there are certain constants: one makes love in the Ukraine or Peking, in New York or New Guinea; one eats, shelters from the cold or heat, and if never quite in the same fashion, the basic needs

189

are always the same. Neanda wants to draw upon information derived from all sources and circumstances, and which will outlive them.

First lesson learned: I proved to those cautious bankers who were sceptical about the success of my enterprise that I was right. Neanda exists just like the big American universities and some foundations do. We've been offered plenty of money. And Neanda's legal constitution ensures that such money belongs to none of us individually: funds are used in accordance with our statutes and requirements. These statutes, for instance, stipulate that fifty one percent of the Nouns and Neads will pay no fees.

Love here, and I mean the only love that counts, doesn't make physical love the slave of wealth or youth, and no longer insists upon beauty for its fulfilment – and is thus no longer condemned to lie.

The aged and infirm, homosexuals, children, the poor and the impotent, whatever the colour of their skins, all have their place in the heptandria which suits them. Of course we too have our right and our left wing, our conservationists, reactionaries, and even our reformers and revolutionaries.

Neanda has no more rediscovered a golden age than it has been able to devise a peaceful future.

Worse still, a small, very small, number of Nouns and Neads will become long-term inhabitants of Neanda. No one will drive them out, however, and so they are assured of a material security as complete as the times allow.

But I mustn't let my ideas and words run away with me: I repeat, then, that Neanda has nothing to do with the young girl whose progress I've recounted. Neanda didn't come into being because of what she lived through.

Nea's life and crime, on the other hand, do concern readers of this book. Inside herself she bore the violence and rebellion we all fall foul of. Her logic and clarity, her virtues, in a word, led her to express so extremely what the conscious mind generally finds so hard to accept.

My father hardly talks any more. He goes for walks. His life is divided between a smaller heptandria he has settled for, and my own, which he visits rather demandingly every so often. Yet he never lays claim to me completely, neither as daughter nor as lover. He only rests a hand on me from time to time or fondles my sex. When I remark on the tears in his eyes he says: 'They're the pearls of memory, souvenirs like pearls. It's not from sorrow, fear, or even love.'

Maurice has resumed and expanded his prisoner's way of life. He's here. We make love less and less together, more and more with others, and we're so alike that many newcomers take us for brother and sister.

The Directress has the job of running things smoothly and she is the one who welcomes the new Nouns and Neads. She chooses them all, men and women, turning away no one. Some of us consider she has a tiresome tendency towards bogus mysticism. She's taken to announcing: 'I am God's whore.' What she means by this is that she is universally available to one and all.

True, she is always ready to jerk off an old man or a young lad floundering about in awkward adolescence. True, she lets girls and women suckle her breasts, and when belly to belly no longer clearly distinguishes penis from clitoris. She only wants, and believes in, a great love. She is a shopgirl not a mystic. She'll never resign herself to giving up her cosmic yearnings. But what an accountant, what an organizer, what an admirable business woman, what a Directress!

As for me, I'm twenty-six and waiting for death.